NEW HAVEN FREE PUBLIC LIBRARY
3 5000 06782 624
P9-CEB-327

T-Backs, T-Shirts, COAT, and Suit

Books By E. L. Konigsburg

Jennifer, Hecate, Macbeth, William McKinley,
and Me, Elizabeth
From the Mixed-Up Files
of Mrs. Basil E. Frankweiler
About the B'Nai Bagels
(George)
Altogether, One at a Time
A Proud Taste for Scarlet and Miniver
The Dragon in the Ghetto Caper
The Second Mrs. Giaconda
Father's Arcane Daughter
Throwing Shadows
Journey to an 800 Number
Up from Jericho Tel
T-backs, T-shirts, COAT, and Suit

Picture Books

Samuel Todd's Book of Great Colors
Samuel Todd's Book of Great Inventions
Amy Elizabeth Explores Bloomingdale's

T-Backs, T-Shirts, COAT, and Suit

E.L. KONIGSBURG

A Jean Karl Book

ATHENEUM 1993 NEW YORK

Maxwell Macmillan Canada
TORONTO
Maxwell Macmillan International
NEW YORK OXFORD SINGAPORE SYDNEY

Atheneum
Macmillan Publishing Company
866 Third Avenue
New York, NY 10022

Maxwell Macmillan Canada, Inc.
1200 Eglinton Avenue East
Suite 200
Don Mills, Ontario M3C 3N1

Macmillan Publishing Company is part of the Maxwell Communication Group of Companies.

First edition
Printed in the United States of America
10 9 8 7 6 5 4 3 2 1
The text of this book is set in 11 point Caledonia

Library of Congress Cataloging-in-Publication Data

Konigsburg, E. L.
T-backs, t-shirts, COAT, and suit / E. L. Konigsburg. —1st ed.
p. cm.
"A Jean Karl book."
Summary: Spending the summer in Florida with her stepfather's sister who operates a "meals-on-wheels" van, twelve-year-old Chloë and her aunt become involved in a controversy surrounding the wearing of T-back bathing suits.
ISBN 0-689-31855-3
[1. Aunts—Fiction. 2. Protest movements—Fiction. 3. Florida—Fiction.] I. Title.
PZ7.K8352Te 1993
[Fic]—dc20 93-18427

To the spirit of Thanksgiving and all its participants—past, present, and future—with love

T-Backs, T-Shirts, COAT, and Suit

In case you live somewhere other than planet Earth and have not heard about T-backs, here is a brief description of them, taken from the law books of the City of Peco, in the State of Florida, U.S.A.

> A T-back is a two-piece bathing suit, the bottom half of which, when seen from the rear, forms a *T*: one strip of cloth around the waist is attached to another strip, centered on the back, covering the crevice of the buttocks but leaving a lot of cheek showing on either side. The front is very much the same as the back except that the vertical strip is wider, and the horizontal dips down. In other words, the T-back makes a V-front. This garment, when worn by women, is most often accompanied by a strapless, low-cut bra. Men wear it topless.

If you have to look up any of the words in this description, if you understand the words but are offended by them, or if you are offended by T-backs themselves, please close this report now, put it back on the shelf, and walk quietly away. They have caused enough trouble already.

Going to Peco for the summer was not Chloë's first choice. Or her second or her third. It was her only choice.

It was when she was asked to sign the hair contract that she knew she had to leave town. Anjelica and Krystal stood over her as she read:

> *We, the undersigned, do hereby agree that if one of us is having a bad hair day, she will call the other undersigneds, and we will all go into the pool together.*

"What happens if you don't?" Chloë asked.

"The others won't speak to you—even over the phone—for the next seven days."

"What happens if you have just been to the beauty parlor for a shampoo, cut, and blow-dry? Do you still have to go into the water?"

"Yes, over the scalp. The deal is total immersion."

Chloë said, "I think you ought to add a clause to that

effect." Anjelica and Krystal agreed that that was a good idea. Anjelica said, "You can sign now, and we'll have everyone initial the clause when we get it typed up. That's the way it's done. I saw it on TV." She held out the pen.

Chloë remembered hearing the proverb, the pen is mightier than the sword, and at that moment she knew why. She felt threatened.

"I would love to sign," she said, "but I can't. I'm not going to be here this summer. It wouldn't be fair of me to sign a contract I cannot honor. It may even be illegal."

When Anjelica and Krystal pressed her about where she would be going over the summer, she said, "It's a surprise."

And that is when Chloë knew that she had to go somewhere if she was not to be shunned—for shunning was the punishment for anyone who refused to sign.

She approached Nick with her problem. "Sleepover camp is out," she said. "It's much too late to enroll me. Much, much too late."

Nick replied, "And you're saying 'thank goodness,' aren't you?" Nick knew that Chloë thought of summer camp as an endless sleepover party, and she was no fan of sleepover parties. She came home from them so grouchy her mother would send her to bed "to wake up better."

"How about going to Florida to spend time with my sister Bernadette?" Nick asked.

"How about my going to Tucson to spend time with Mother's sister, Aunt Helena?" Chloë countered.

"Your Aunt Helena is planning a cruise of the fjords in Norway this summer. I think you should spend some time with Bernadette."

Chloë said, "I could go on the cruise with Aunt Helena. Do you think she would mind taking me along?"

"Yes, I do. I think she would mind a great deal—even if we could afford it and even if there were time to include you. I think you should spend time with my sister Bernadette."

The more Nick thought about it, the more he knew that was where Chloë should be. Chloë and his sister should get to know each other. More than that, the time was right for them to do so. Right for both of them.

Chloë said, "Too bad I don't have any grandparents who live out of town. They'd take me."

Nick replied, "Let's hope that Bernadette will." He looked at Chloë's worried face, smiled, and said, "If I ask, she will. It may take some coaxing, but she'll do it."

Chloë had met Bernadette only once. That was when she had come to Nick's wedding. She had served as Nick's best man and had worn a tuxedo and flats. Chloë remembered that her hair was short—short enough to comb with a suede brush—and that she was tall. Even in flats she had towered over every other woman at the wedding. If Nick himself weren't exceptionally tall, she would have towered over him too.

Before he made the call, Nick said he would make the arrangements only if Chloë promised to help Bernadette. Chloë thought that sounded a little bit like blackmail, but she was not in a position to bargain, so she agreed not only to spend time with this person she had seen only once but also to help her. If it weren't for Bernadette, it would be total immersion and the hair contract.

Bernadette agreed—reluctantly—to take Chloë for a few weeks.

Bernadette had raised Nick. When he insisted that Chloë go to Florida, Nick didn't know that the T-back war would break out, but he knew his sister, and he knew Chloë, and he knew they needed each other. Whatever happened over the summer, it was time for their lives to touch.

2

Since there had been no time to buy a hospitality present, at the airport Chloë's mother gave her a crisp, new fifty-dollar bill and told her to buy something special for Bernadette. "Look things over. Use your judgment. See if there is something she needs for the house."

* * *

The stewardess took Chloë to a seat in the bulkhead, the first row of the coach section. She made certain that Chloë was buckled in and then left to tend to other passengers coming on board.

Chloë was alone. More alone than she had ever been in her entire life. More alone than she had been in the years before her mother had married Nick and she had been left at day care.

Here she was, breaking away from her mother, Nick, her two best friends, and Ridgewood, New Jersey. Here she was, attached only to the seat of the plane, about to leave the very earth itself, with not a single person around who knew that she considered *total immersion* the two most frightening words in the English language.

With neither friend nor phone around, Chloë decided to think. She decided to think about death. She could possibly be very close to it. Planes were known to crash regardless of who was on board. She wondered if twelve-year-olds who die in airplane crashes get to grow up in heaven or do they stay twelve forever. She wondered if they ever get to have sex, or do they only get to watch it down on earth. She decided that they must have sex up in heaven, because nowadays they needed angels to beget angels since no one on earth seemed capable of becoming one.

Having solved that, she smiled to herself.

It was wonderful, having all this time alone. At home there was so much to think about that she never had time to. Having solved the major problem of death, she was ready to think about life. But the woman who came to occupy the seat next to hers started a conversation, and once Chloë started talking, all thinking stopped. She was sorry to have to stop thinking because she had enjoyed it.

After the initial questions about where she was going and why, the woman started talking about her perfect oldest granddaughter, named Heather. Helplessly strapped into her seat, Chloë was being shown an entire pocket-sized photo album of pictures of Heather atop a horse, wearing a red jacket and a peaked riding hat. The horse, like Heather, was a champion. Chloë said that near her home in Ridgewood there was some fine horse-riding country. "Jackie O. rides there," she added.

Heather's grandmother replied that the finest horse

country is in Virginia. Chloë said, "The people who run the Kentucky Derby don't think so."

There was still an hour and half to go on the flight, and Chloë was tired of Heather's grandmother. She wanted to be flung through the heavens, strapped to her seat, all alone with time to think. Being Heather's grandmother—or anybody's grandmother for that matter—didn't give that person the right to interrupt another person's thinking, even if the thinking person was twelve.

"There are famous horsewomen in my family," Chloë said. "We are descendants of Joan of Arc."

Heather's grandmother said, "But Joan of Arc was burned at the stake as a heretic. She never married. She never had any children."

Chloë said, "Yes, that's true. But she had three brothers."

"But that is not a direct line of descent."

"It's good enough for royalty."

"What did you say your name was?"

"Pollack. P-O-L-L-A-C-K. If you know anything at all about ethnic names, you know that it is an abbreviated version of Paul-of-Arc. My father Nick has the mark of the Arcs on his left shoulder." Chloë drew a picture of Nick's tattoo on the back of one of Heather's pictures. "You can see it resembles a bow and arrow. Everyone in his family has that mark somewhere on the body."

Nick did have a small tattoo of the peace symbol on his left shoulder. He had gotten it when he lived in a commune called Spinach Hill. Everyone who lived there got the peace symbol tattooed somewhere. It seemed like a good idea at the time.

When Anjelica and Krystal saw Nick's tattoo, they asked if Nick had been in the Navy—they had heard that sailors often got tattoos and Nick's looked like an anchor, sort of. Chloë told them yes. She did not care to share the information about Nick's life in the commune with them, even though she herself loved hearing about it.

The commune had been a big old house called Spinach Hill, just outside the Peco city limits. No one knew why it was called Spinach Hill. There was no hill, and no one grew spinach, but it was a time when everyone was into naming things. The commune people named their kitchen stove *Phillip* and their lawn mower *Gretel.* Nick's sister, Bernadette, had an old VW bug; she named it Lillian. No reason except that it seemed like a good idea at the time. Besides naming everything, the residents of Spinach Hill were *into* peace, love, understanding, and protests against everyone who was not into peace, love, and understanding. All of them were also into ending the war in Vietnam. Thus the great interest in peace symbols.

The members put their earnings into a joint account and took turns cleaning, cooking, mowing the lawn, and doing house repairs. They were into sharing. That part sounded an awful lot like summer camp to Chloë.

Fourteen people lived in the commune. Twelve were college drop-outs. Bernadette was the only one who had not gone to college at all. She was also the only one who was responsible for a kid brother. Nick was that kid brother. They lived at Spinach Hill for a year. Chloë was now the age that Nick had been when he lived there with Bernadette.

* * *

Heather's grandmother put her pictures away and said, "You shouldn't write on other people's property."

"You won't regret what I've done," Chloë said. "You can save or sell that photo because by placing the mark of Arc on it, I've made it quite valuable."

Heather's grandmother didn't say another word until they were served dinner, and then she complained about the food.

"If you think you are going to vomit, please use the barf bag," Chloë said, pointing to the seat pocket on the wall facing them. "You'll save us both a lot of embarrassment and dry cleaning."

Heather's grandmother said nothing else for the remainder of the flight, but Chloë couldn't get back to the deep thinking she had been doing before she was interrupted.

* * *

The airline attendant stood at the mouth of the plane and said good-bye to every single other passenger before she came back for Chloë. Chloë got hot and sweaty. She could feel her hair starting to frizz. She certainly wasn't going to make a good impression on Bernadette feeling hot and looking frizzy. She unzipped her vest pocket to make sure that her money was still there. The fifty-dollar bill was no longer crisp. It actually felt hot. She could not remember ever having paper money feel hot before. Her first conclusion about spending a summer in Florida was: No more vests—dressing in layers was out. The second was: If Bernadette did not have air-conditioning, she might have to use the fifty dollars to make other arrangements. A hotel room was not above her means.

At last the stewardess came for her. As she emerged

from the jetway, she saw Bernadette standing with the people remaining. Nick had shown her some recent pictures of his sister to refresh her memory, but what she remembered of her—that she was a tall person—would have been enough. Bernadette stood above the crowd.

Bernadette was a full six feet tall, as skinny as a silhouette, pale as a glass of buttermilk, and so nearsighted that her eyeglasses could be sent into orbit to do the job of the Hubble space telescope. She wore a long, full, printed skirt with a drawstring waist, sandals, and a dark T-shirt that didn't have anything printed on it. She had a head of unruly silver-and-black curly hair that grew in several directions, only one of which was down. It looked as if you could stuff a mattress—king-size—with it. Chloë wondered if this woman ever had a good hair day.

The airline attendant would not give Bernadette custody until she showed a picture ID. Bernadette took out her driver's license. As the stewardess looked at the picture, Chloë looked at the numbers—the last two were the year of her birth. Bernadette was forty-five. Chloë thought, No wonder she has so much gray in her hair.

They greeted each other with smiles but did not hug or kiss. They did not even kiss the air over each other's shoulders as grown-ups often do.

As they walked toward baggage pickup, Bernadette said, "I'll call you Chloë." Chloë found that a strange thing for an almost-relative to say. *Chloë* was, after all, her name. When her name was to be written, Chloë insisted that the two dots be placed over the *e*. She loved having two dots over the *e* of her name and told everyone that they were called a *diaeresis* and meant that both the *o* and the *e* were to be sounded. Even before she started first grade she would not allow anyone to skip her diaeresis. Everyone called her Chloë. No one shortened it to Chlo. Why would this woman think of calling her anything but Chloë?

It would be no use telling this person, who was stuck with the same last name, that it was *Pollack* that she was considering dropping as soon as she came of age or got married—whichever came first. There was always the possibility of hyphenating her last name with her husband's, but she already had two last names.

Nick had adopted Chloë when she was five, a year after he married her mother. When they drew up the adoption papers, they tucked her birth father's last name between her new last name and her two given names, and she became Chloë June Parker Pollack. If she used all four of her names, she would run out of spaces on credit-card applications, so except for contracts and report cards, she was simply called Chloë Pollack.

As they walked farther along the concourse, Bernadette said, "You call me Bernadette. *Aunt* won't be necessary. And I don't like Bernie. Or Aunt Bernie or Auntie. For a while, when I was twelve, I wanted everyone to call me Detta. No reason except that I was twelve and trying to fit whatever name seemed more glamorous than Bernadette. I like to be called Bernadette. I've become my name."

"All right," Chloë said, feeling very much the grown-up in this conversation. "Chloë and Bernadette. That's what it will be for our time remaining." *Time remaining* sounded like a grown-up thing to say. She thought she was beginning to understand why Nick had asked her to help this person.

3

Bernadette drove to her house in her black '76 Pontiac Firebird. The hood ornament was the head of a bird, and fanning out behind it was the painting of a firebird, the phoenix, with its tail circling right and left in a pattern of red, orange, and yellow flames. Much too garish for Ridgewood, Chloë thought. Not in good taste. Rather childish.

The car was very clean. Exceptionally clean. Spotless, in fact. She knew that Nick would not send her to anyplace that was not clean, but she wondered if he had remembered the health dangers of secondary smoke. Chloë reached toward the ashtray to see if there were any telltale signs of cigarette butts.

"I don't smoke," Bernadette said.

Embarrassed at having her thoughts read, Chloë said, "I must compliment you on the cleanliness of your car. A person could do brain surgery in here."

"I love this car," Bernadette said. "Do all the work on it myself. Probably spend as much time under the hood as behind the wheel. I am so familiar with it, I can change its plugs, oil, and bearings blindfolded." She glanced at Chloë and smiled.

Chloë watched Bernadette's smile. Chloë read smiles the way some people read tea leaves or tarot cards. The most important thing she watched for was how it grew. *Slow* and *twitchy* were the two basic styles. Female salesclerks and office receptionists had twitchy smiles for twelve-year-old females. Dental hygienists, wonderful slow smiles; fast-food waiters, twitchy; actors playing fast-food waiters on TV, slow. Anchorpersons, two basic smiles: twitchy-twitchy when they were talking to each other and slow-twitchy when they were delivering animal stories.

Bernadette's smile took its time. It was, Chloë decided, exactly like Nick's. Not twitchy. Not nervous. It was, in fact, a beautiful smile. Bernadette's teeth were even and white, almost translucent, like milk.

Bernadette said, "If you like my Firebird, wait until you see Daisy, my dog. She's black, too." Then Bernadette turned on the car radio to the classical music station and conversation stopped.

Chloë had not been told there was a dog. She did not understand dogs or people who did. Big dogs always had their tongues out, and small ones were yippy. She pretended to like them when she went to the mall with Anjelica and Krystal, and they stopped by the pet store to browse. Chloë didn't mind any animal that was safely behind bars, but the truth was, it was only in the movies that she found them adorable. She didn't care for anything—including humans—with too much facial or body hair, and she failed to see the difference between animals in the wild and animals as pets. They were equally unembarrassed about performing certain bodily functions in public. But she never admitted that to anyone—*anyone*—especially Anjelica, who had a brother in Greenpeace, and Krystal, who actually taped all the *National Geographic* specials on PBS.

When they got to the house, Chloë met the dog. It was big, and it was black, and it seemed no more anxious to meet her than she was to meet it. It stood still, close to Bernadette's side, staring. After Bernadette made soft, clucking sounds, it approached Chloë, sniffing as it approached. Whichever parts were not covered with hair appeared to be excessively moist. Chloë did not want to be slobbered or shed upon. She pulled her arms in close to her sides to make herself as small a target as possible. "Are you going to tell me that I shouldn't show fear?" she asked.

Bernadette said, "It's a good idea not to."

"Fine," Chloë said, "because what I'm feeling is terror."

"She's really very gentle."

"That's what they all say."

Bernadette made more soft, clucking noises in its direction, and it finally lifted its head. It wanted something. Bernadette said, "You can pet her now."

Chloë replied, "Must I?"

Bernadette said, "Of course not. But Daisy will remember that she offered herself to you, and you refused."

Chloë thought, I better. So she touched the top of its head with the tips of her fingers. It was not hot or oily but was, in fact, cool and clean-feeling, so she laid her whole palm flat on its back somewhere below its collar. With only that slight pressure on its back, it sat at her feet. She stroked a short section of its back between its collar and tail. She would not be too friendly; dogs kissed by licking, and she did not want to experience dog saliva on any of her body parts or find dog hairs on any of her possessions. The thought of finding dog hairs on her toothbrush made her shudder.

Bernadette called it back to her side and said that they better call Nick and tell him that she had arrived safely.

Chloë's mother got on one of the extensions and Nick on another. Bernadette handed Chloë the phone. Chloë thought that Bernadette would get on one of her other phones so that they could have a four-way conversation, but she didn't. It wasn't until later that Chloë realized that Bernadette had only one phone in her entire house. And it was a wall-mounted rotary dial.

Her parents were very glad to hear from her, and just before hanging up, Nick said, "Chloë?"

She knew he wanted to say something important, and she was not in the mood.

"Chloë?"

"What?"

"Chloë, will you promise me that you'll help Bernadette?"

"She has a dog."

Nick laughed. "So you've met Daisy."

"You knew there was a dog?"

Nick laughed again. "Just promise me something. Promise me that you'll help Bernadette and that you'll give the unexpected a chance."

"That's not *some* thing. That's *two* things."

"Just promise me those two things."

Chloë sighed. "It's awful hot here. . . . My hair is . . . and . . . Oh! All right."

Nick said, "Chloë, darling, I think you're going to do just fine. Just fine."

* * *

Bernadette asked if she needed help unpacking. Chloë said no. "I am not a person you will have to remind to wash, floss, brush, or flush either."

Bernadette said, "Good," and then announced, "I am going to my room now. Once I retire to my room, you must not enter, and you must not bother me until morning except for an emergency."

Chloë thought, Why is she telling me this? Does she think I want to climb into her bed and cuddle? I am not a person who climbs into strangers' beds unless I am in a hotel and the sheets are clean.

Bernadette continued, "You can play the television after I've gone to my room, but if you must, use these." She handed Chloë a pair of earphones. "Daisy sleeps in my room."

Chloë thought, That's a relief.

Then Bernadette said, "We get up at five-thirty."

"Five-thirty? A.M.?"

Bernadette nodded.

"Why?" she asked, thinking Bernadette wanted them up early so they could make the three-hour drive to Disney World.

"Work," Bernadette replied.

"And second choice is . . . ?"

"There is no second choice."

Chloë thought, That's been the story of my life this summer. "Five-thirty, then," she said.

"I'll shower in the morning and waken you as soon as I'm dressed," Bernadette said and went to her bedroom. Without being asked, the dog followed.

Chloë watched it. She thought, I don't know much about dogs, but I wonder if this one is a cyborg. Bernadette had said that it was a Lab. Could that possibly mean *Laboratory*? No human dog could be that obedient. What had Bernadette done to make it so?

* * *

There was a chair, a bed, and a chest of drawers in the room that was to be hers. Everything—even the floor—was painted white. The only color in the room came from a quilt made of tiny squares the size of postage stamps and a cobalt-blue glass vase full of fresh wildflowers that was on top of the dresser. Chloë thought, Nice touch! There was no mirror anywhere in the room. Not even on the back of the closet door. She would have to do her hair in the bathroom. Chloë thought, Not so nice.

She unpacked and laid out her clothes for the next day. She always carefully planned her day's wardrobe. She chose clean underwear, jeans, the long-sleeved turquoise shirt with the white ribbed collar and cuffs, matching socks, new Nikes, and the heavy leather belt with the silver-and-turquoise trim. (Not real silver and not real turquoise but an excellent copy.) And the turquoise headband.

She lined up her other shoes on the floor of the closet, hung up her blouses so that all the hangers faced the same way, and placed her folded underpants in the drawer in a row so straight and precise that they looked like the lingerie counter at Bloomingdale's. She stood back and admired her work. She then folded up the fifty-dollar bill until it was the size of a quarter and put it in the pocket of the ivory linen-and-acetate dress and pinned the pocket shut. She had bought the dress before she knew she was coming to Bernadette's. She had never worn it—the price tag still dangled from the sleeve—but she could tell already that she would have little occasion to wear it in Peco, Florida.

After taking a bath, Chloë walked through the rest of the house. She would look things over and see what she could buy that would be a suitable hospitality gift.

The house was plain. Spotless but plain. No dining room. Only two bedrooms. The living room served as family room and library. There was a row of encyclopedias underneath the window seat. Only one TV and one bathroom. Of course, she thought, who knows what—besides the dog—lurks in Bernadette's room. There were two air conditioners that looked like steamer trunks stuck in the windows, dripping water from their backsides into the yard, and there were two signs of the modern age—a Cuisinart and a small electric coffee mill—in the kitchen.

Chloë folded down the postage-stamp quilt, moving from one side of the bed to the other so that she could smooth each fold and make the corners match. She climbed between the crisp, white sheets and lay flat and still.

She felt almost as alone as she had felt on the plane before Heather's grandmother had appeared. She began the thinking process again. She wanted to think about life, not her life, but life itself, but instead she kept thinking about Bernadette: How did she know that the dog would remember that I didn't pet it? That was strange. But then Bernadette was strange.

Her house was strange: plain but stylish, and so was she. Bernadette had those high cheekbones that all the fashion magazines say are the first thing they look for in models. Chloë thought, With contacts and a good make-over, she could be an attractive older woman, even with the impossible hair, of which she had grown quite a crop since the wedding.

At the last slumber party she had gone to, the entertainment for the evening was to practice doing make-overs, even though no one was allowed to wear makeup yet, so they were not exactly make-*overs*. Neither Krystal nor Chloë participated. Krystal said she didn't need any practice because she soon would be actually wearing makeup, since her mother would allow it as soon as she had to shave her armpits. Krystal didn't lift her arms once all night. Chloë resisted doing the make-overs by saying she had a cold and didn't want anyone to have to share her lipstick. The truth was she had no cold but she didn't want to share a lipstick, so for the rest of the night she pretended to have the sniffles.

She thought about all the slumber parties she would miss over the summer. What a relief. When she was nine and ten years old, they had been fun, but lately—ever since sixth grade—they weren't. You were invited to come as yourself, and yet you were expected to be like everyone else once you got there. So you either had to pretend you were like everyone else or pretend you had a cold.

Chloë snuggled farther down between the sheets, which smelled like a combination of Clorox and the out-of-doors, and thought about a possible hospitality gift: Does Bernadette know that there are any number of colors and patterns available in bed linens nowadays, or is there simply no place in Peco where a person can buy them?

4

At a quarter after six the next morning they were in the Firebird and on their way to work. Bernadette parked outside a building that looked like a metal tent. Over the door was a sign that said ZACK'S MEALS-ON-WHEELS in big, bold letters. Underneath, in smaller letters it said: WAREHOUSE AND COMMISSARY. Bernadette got out of the car and went to a van that had ZACK'S MEALS-ON-WHEELS printed on its side. She unlocked the van and drove it the short distance to a loading dock.

They went inside the warehouse.

Mountains of cardboard containers lined the walls. More cartons than Chloë had ever seen, even in a wholesale club. They were full of soft drinks, snacks, paper cups, plates and napkins and straws and wooden stirrers. Across the floor there was a brightly lighted section that looked like the cafeteria at school. Two women wearing tissue-paper hats stood behind a counter making sandwiches and wrapping them.

Bernadette filled two chests with ice and one with dry

ice. Then she loaded up with raw hamburgers, hot dogs, two kinds of buns, slaw, sausages, sauerkraut, coffee, cream, sugar, two kinds of artificial sweeteners, iced tea, mustard, relish, ketchup and onions, potato chips, pretzels, pork rinds, candy bars, and dozens of the wrapped sandwiches. Everything was either tucked or clipped into place, and everything was counted and listed on a clipboard as she loaded it.

"We have to return either with the food or the money for it," she explained as she signed the clipboard. "I get paid a percentage of what I take in. The more I sell, the more money I make."

"Who buys this stuff?" Chloë asked.

"People who work out-of-doors or in places where there are no restaurants nearby."

They would come under the category of the unexpected. Chloë had never met a working adult who didn't have an office. Except Bernadette.

They were loaded up, ready to go, when Zack of Zack's Meals-on-Wheels came out of a far corner of the warehouse. He was a hairy man. Chloë expected his knuckles to graze the ground as he walked toward them.

Bernadette introduced Chloë. "This is Nick's kid," she said.

"Well, well, well," he said. His voice sounded like tires that were low on air slowly rolling over gravel. He asked Bernadette what she intended to do with "the kid" while she was running her route.

Bernadette replied, "Not *the kid,* Zack. This is Nick's kid." Then she said that she planned on taking Chloë with her. "I figure if she does half the work, I get half a vacation."

Zack said, "If you weren't my oldest employee, Bernadette, I wouldn't let you."

Bernadette said, "Do you know what he means by oldest employee, Chloë?"

She said, "Of course I do. He means that you were born before anyone else who works here."

Bernadette laughed. "That's true only on the days Grady Oates doesn't show up."

Zack snickered. "Your aunt has been with me longer than anyone else who works for me. She's the best in the business."

Bernadette winked. "You know, Chloë, it ain't bragging if it's true."

As soon as Bernadette had backed the van out of the loading dock, another, smaller van pulled in. Bernadette waved to the man behind the wheel. "That," she said, "is Grady Oates. He drives the only van that doesn't serve hot food. He services the discount malls out on the interstate. They don't open until ten, so Grady doesn't come to work until those of us who serve hot food have already loaded up. Grady is also the only person who uses his van as a family car. Except that Grady has no family. He lives alone. He's a Vietnam vet. Lost a leg in the war."

"Which leg?"

"His left. Doesn't interfere with his driving."

"All the way up to his crotch?"

"No, just to the knee."

"How many vans does Zack own?"

"Eight, including Grady's. But he also owns the commissary, and it supplies the food for two other companies—one of them takes hot meals to shut-ins. It's important to get to the commissary early to get a good variety of stuff. Soup is hot stuff in the winter."

Chloë got the joke but was in no mood to laugh. Sweat was happening already.

Bernadette headed out to Talleyrand. Talleyrand is a three-mile stretch along the Heartfelt River where docks and warehouses line the riverfront. There are also two dry docks for ship repairs. Some ships come in for repairs; others come to load and unload. In a single day, automobiles from Japan and Germany, bananas from Costa Rica, and oil from Venezuela come to be unloaded. The street across from the docks is lined with stores selling ship supplies and warehouses for storage. Talleyrand is the oldest part of town. One of the side streets off Talleyrand is paved with bricks instead of asphalt. The buildings on both sides are weathered and gray, and the roofs look rusty.

For Zack's Meals-on-Wheels, Talleyrand was the best beat. It had to be serviced twice: once at morning break and again at lunch. Competition among food service vans was tough. In all of Peco, there were forty-six mobile units working out of eighteen commissaries. Sometimes there were as many as nine of them at Talleyrand.

Zack himself sent two and sometimes three vans there, depending on how busy the docks and shipyards were. He sent others to various spots around town where apartments or malls were being built, and one van went forty-five miles south to where major repairs were being done on the interstate; that was the worst beat and was always given to the newest employee. Not only did the driver have to drive miles and miles to get there, but there were some days when the weather did not allow the road crews to work at all.

By the time Chloë arrived in Peco, Bernadette had been working for Zack for seven years. Zack's business had grown in the seven years she had been there, and she had helped it grow. She had earned Talleyrand.

Bernadette didn't do anything slowly. She moved like an Olympic skier, zigzagging around and alongside obstacles but never stopping her forward motion. The space in the back of the van was hardly big enough for two people. Chloë was told that the board of health did spot checks and could close them down if everything wasn't clean. Besides keeping things clean, they had to keep everything in its place. There was no place for it, except in its place.

Chloë approved.

Bernadette taught her how to chop onions as they drove to the first stop. It was hot and close in the back of the van, and she had to work fast, making it even hotter. Chloë thought she would drown in her own sweat. It poured from her brow, from under her arms and belt, and from behind her knees. Tears blinded her eyes as she chopped the onions. Lot's wife was not as salty as she was. Neither was the Atlantic nor the Pacific. Between the sweat and the tears, she was being pickled in her very own brine.

Bernadette paid no attention to Chloë. She was too busy getting to the best spot on Talleyrand. The best spot was exactly opposite the gate to the docks. There the men would see her van first as they came out for their break. Within seconds of her parking, other vans pulled up in front of her and in back of her.

Bernadette next taught Chloë how to jump down out of the van, open the window, pull down the ledge, put up the awning, and set out what Bernadette liked to call her condiments. Bernadette could do all that with a single sweeping motion, but she was a tall person, a very tall person, an *experienced* very tall person. Chloë was inexperienced. And short. And had to reach farther and pull harder. Her arms felt stretched like bungee ropes, and her hands bounced here and there as she set out the mustard, the relish, the ketchup, and the onions that she had so recently chopped and cried over.

Bernadette paid no attention to Chloë's discomfort and pain.

She blew a wooden whistle that she wore on a leather thong around her neck. Chloë asked if she thought the men could hear that little whistle over the clang of hammers and the noise of welding torches.

Bernadette told her that even if the men could not hear it, the drug-sniffing dogs could. "They send up a howl that no one can ignore. The men know I'm here."

And, sure enough, the workers started coming.

Bernadette watched them approach and began to slaw dogs and run mustard over burgers even as they walked toward her. She knew which of her customers wanted cream in his coffee and which wanted one sugar and which wanted two. She could pour coffee with one hand and spread mayonnaise with the other and not splash, spill, or drip a drop.

There were some women working in the offices and a few who worked the docks, but most of Bernadette's customers were men. Macho men. Bernadette knew how to joke around with them. The guys joked back but never crossed the line between playful talk and dirty talk. Bernadette told Chloë that the important thing to remember was that the customer is always right, and then, every now and then, to remind him how you define *right*.

Three of Bernadette's regular customers didn't like drinking out of Styrofoam cups, so Bernadette kept china mugs for them. She wrote their names on the mugs with red fingernail polish and kept them in the glove compartment in the front of the van. One of the men didn't have cash with him, but Bernadette served him anyway. "He'll be by on payday asking me what he owes. He knows—they all know—that if they don't pay Bernadette, Bernadette still has to pay Zack. It wouldn't take the fingers of one hand to count the times I've gotten stiffed."

All morning they moved from the docks to the shipyards to the ship chandlers across the street. When there was a break from serving customers, they were busy unwrapping meat patties and making more coffee and cleaning, cleaning, straightening, straightening, and sweat kept happening.

Noon found them back at the docks. Some of the workers carried their lunches but bought cold drinks from Bernadette. "Don't they have a Coke machine in that place?" Chloë asked.

"Bite your tongue," Bernadette said. "Coke machines are the enemy. Actually, a lot of the office workers just like to take a break in the fresh air."

"Fresh air!" Chloë said. "Fresh air, you say? You call this fresh air?" she asked, waving her arms over her head. "In Ridgewood what we call air is a gas and is full of *O*-

two, oxygen." She waved her arms over her head again. "This is not even a gas. This is rain that is just too stupid to fall."

Bernadette laughed. "You'll get used to it."

Chloë thought, Not in your lifetime. Nick asked me to help, he didn't ask me to lay down my life. When we get back to the house, I'm going to use that fifty dollars to make other arrangements.

Then another wave of workers came by, and she got so busy chopping, pouring, and spreading, that she had no time to think about sweat or making other arrangements.

* * *

By two o'clock they were done on Talleyrand. Bernadette put the van in gear and pulled away from the curb. "Help yourself to anything we have left," she said.

Chloë asked, "Is that lunch?"

Bernadette said, "Yes."

"What about you? Aren't you going to eat?"

"I would appreciate an egg-salad sandwich," she said.

"There's a couple of hamburgers left. I'll split them with you."

"I don't eat anything that has a face or comes from something that did," she replied.

"Eggs come from something that had a face."

"There is this important difference: You don't have to kill the chicken to get the eggs."

"What would you like to drink with that egg salad?" Chloë asked.

"A Coke would be fine."

"Diet or Classic?"

"Classic."

"Cup or straw?"

Bernadette looked over at Chloë long enough for her to watch the full slow-motion blossoming of a smile. "Only one day on the job, and you're a pro. Nick said you were a quick study."

What else had Nick said? Chloë decided that she would find out later when she discussed her working conditions. In the meantime, she decided to let Bernadette enjoy her egg-salad sandwich.

* * *

Bernadette headed out to the beach where a high-rise luxury hotel, the Ritz, was being built. Even in Ridgewood, Chloë had never seen anything like it. It was bigger than the Hanover Mall. Fancier than Neiman Marcus, Victoria's Secret, and Bloomingdale's put together, and there were certainly going to be a lot more bathrooms. Bernadette called it "the mother of all hotels."

The Ritz was so far out of town that it was not on any of the regular van routes, so all these workers carried their lunches. The men worked in crews according to their specialties. Electricians and plumbers, tile men and drywall men and carpenters, all worked at different spots around the gigantic shell that spread out over the whole oceanfront and cast a shadow as big as cloud cover. Bernadette didn't have to blow her whistle because the men who saw her first sent out a call that was picked up by the next batch, and they sent it to the next ones, and so on and so on.

None of the other van operators would be stopping at the Ritz. Drivers who had been working for Zack for a long time always pulled in a little extra stop. Marie stopped at the condos being built at Crossroads; Lionel, the apartments near the University; and Wanda, the school construction site on Kings Road. The Ritz was a nice extra for one van, but two wouldn't make it worth the time it took to get there. Zack didn't mind drivers making extra stops as long as they didn't get back late for check-in. The more they sold, the more money he made.

Bernadette showed the carpenters her wooden whistle and told them that her brother Nick had carved it. And then she did something she had not done on Talleyrand: She introduced Chloë to the carpenters' crew. "These are craftsmen," she explained. "They appreciate fine work." The men admired the whistle, and Bernadette mentioned that Nick had trained himself to work with wood.

Chloë had forgotten that Nick liked to work with wood. He had not done it in a long time. On the day he had married her mother, Nick had given Chloë a little box he had made. "A wedding present for you," he had said. The carved wooden box had once been her favorite possession, but she had not thought about it in a long time.

She kept barrettes in it, but in sixth grade she stopped using them. Starting in sixth grade, girls let their hair fall in their faces or pushed it back by shaking their heads. There was a technique to it. You tilt your head on the side opposite the part, then jerk your head back with a slight twist. Chloë practiced in front of a mirror before she tried her technique in public. The most important thing about hair-tossing was not to get the frizzies. Frizzy hair never tossed right. On a list of possible bad hair days, *frizzy* was at the top.

Instead of buying sandwiches and coffee, the men of the Ritz bought a lot of pretzels and chips and gallons of Gatorade.

Chloë wondered, Does everything taste the same to

everyone, and likes and dislikes are different, or do things really taste different to different people?

Bernadette must have been reading her mind because she said, "I don't know if these men have different tastes or not, but I do know they need salt. They sweat so much."

"*They* sweat!" Chloë said. "What about what is happening to me? I have not mentioned it, Bernadette, but I am dripping wet."

Bernadette said, "I noticed."

Just then Chloë felt sweat trickle down her leg. She hated that. She said, "I think you should know, Bernadette, that I am not fond of having my body fluids soak through my clothing. My pants are so wet, someone who does not know me might think I had urinated in them."

"You shouldn't have worn that stuff," Bernadette said. "The minute I saw you come out this morning, I thought so."

"You could have said something."

"I'm saying it now. Tomorrow, wear shorts or a skirt, like me. One of the myths about jeans is that they are the most comfortable clothes in the world. Not always. And wear sandals. Why don't you take that headband from around your hair and put it over your forehead to keep the sweat out of your eyes the way I do with my kerchief." Bernadette checked her watch. "Let's go down to the beach. That will cool you off."

Bernadette locked up the van, and together they climbed over heaps of cement and around the huge pit that would be the swimming pool. There, on the other side of the rubble, was the beach and all its elements: sun, sea, salt, sand, and the breeze that whipped them together. And there, beyond the pink ribbon of sand, was the Atlantic Ocean, kissing the sky just as God had asked it to. It sparkled and winked in the sun, inviting Chloë in.

She pulled off her Nikes and ran to the edge of the water and felt the sea breeze unfurl the film of sweat in one long, seamless sweep. Then she turned to Bernadette and thanked her.

Bernadette told her to dive in. "Go ahead," she said. "We have time."

Chloë shook her head.

"Nobody here says you have to have a bathing suit to go bathing. You'll dry off by the time we get home."

Chloë shook her head again.

"Doesn't that water look good to you?" Bernadette asked.

"Not especially," Chloë answered.

"Would swimming lessons make it look any better?"

Chloë nodded yes.

Bernadette checked her watch again. "We'll start tomorrow," she said.

5

Chloë didn't know how she got through that first week except that she had promised Nick to help and to welcome the unexpected, and during that first week, it seemed that everything that wasn't work was unexpected.

There was not a minute from the time she got up until she went to bed when she wasn't busy. Every evening after checking back into the commissary, they rushed home. Chloë pulled off her sweat-soaked clothes and put on her bathing suit while Bernadette let the dog out to do its business. Then they immediately got back into the car and drove out to Seminole, the beach nearest Bernadette's house.

Bernadette said they had to pick up the dog. "Daisy loves the beach," she said. "It would upset her to know that we went without her."

Chloë didn't understand, but she was getting used to hearing things like that from Bernadette. And the dog did love the beach, all right. The minute Bernadette stopped the car, the dog went ballistic. It pushed open the door as soon as Bernadette released the handle, and leaped out. Not scratching Bernadette's beloved Firebird as it left was the only well-mannered thing it did until it got back in. It raced into the surf, came back on shore, rolled in the sand, and made three or four runs before Bernadette and Chloë even made it to the edge of water.

At first, Chloë didn't go in any deeper than the tidewater pools that were left by the receding tide. They were shallow and warm and as comfortable as a bath. She lay down on her stomach and then flipped over onto her back. She didn't even try to soak up the last slant rays of sun that might give her a tan. The first two afternoons, she did nothing but wallow.

On the third day, she stood by Bernadette's side at the water's edge. She dug her toes into the sand and licked salt off her lips and said nothing. Bernadette let her stand by her side for a few minutes and then, without being asked, took her hand and waded out into the water up to her waist. She supported Chloë at the midriff and started to teach her how to swim.

That day and the next, she showed Chloë how to move her arms and turn her head on alternate strokes. Then she taught her how to kick from the hips to get a good forward motion. She taught her one thing at a time, knowing exactly when each small fear was conquered. Secretly and slowly, with Bernadette as her teacher, without either Anjelica or Krystal to see her flounder, Chloë learned to swim.

Bernadette unrolled her hair and waded into the water, but she never put on a bathing suit and never swam. Once a wave swept up suddenly and broke over her head, and she got soaking wet. She smiled, wrung out the hem of her skirt, and tossed her head to shake the water from it. Other days, she came out of the water, her skirt sticking to her like a bodysuit, and she would let it drip. She never seemed to mind getting her clothes soaking wet, but she never put on a bathing suit.

And the way she taught swimming was unexpected, for although she seemed to know everything about swimming and about how to teach it, she never allowed her feet not to touch bottom. Never once did she venture into the water to a depth where the soles of her feet left the sand.

Chloë asked Bernadette point-blank if she knew how to swim.

She answered, "Enough to save you if I want to."

Chloë asked if she would ever go in swimming with her, and she answered, "No," loud and clear. When asked why, she replied, "To spare you and the world that sight." After that, Chloë stopped asking. She knew that whatever reasons Bernadette had, fear was not one.

* * *

On that first exhausting day when they got back from work, Chloë was ready to take a cool shower and collapse in front of the TV and watch Oprah, but something else unexpected happened.

Bernadette said, "Since we'll be going back to the beach tomorrow, Daisy and I better do some gardening today." She called the dog, and the two of them left by the back door.

Chloë had never met a dog who gardened.

She was curious. She followed.

The air was so humid that the backyard felt as if God

had turned on a giant vaporizer for a world full of asthma sufferers. Everything was plumped out. Leaves that looked ordinary in Ridgewood looked as if they had silicone implants here.

Chloë watched Bernadette and the dog wander out to the field behind the house. The dog stopped, still as a statue, and stared. Bernadette stopped too. She stooped down, picked something up, examined it, and put it in a basket. Twice, she threw it away. Whenever she put something in the basket, she patted the dog and said, "Good girl."

Chloë came closer.

Mushrooms!

Bernadette was putting wild mushrooms in the basket, and the dog was helping her find them.

They walked back to the garden, where Bernadette picked some flowers before returning to the house. She washed her harvest, put it into a salad bowl, and tossed the mushrooms and flowers together with spinach and lettuce.

"Is this what they call a *garden salad*?" Chloë asked.

Bernadette nodded. "I grow borage and pansies, nasturtiums and violets especially for salads. And hyssops too. The leaves of hyssop make a wonderful tea. I sweeten it with honey and drink it when I have a sore throat. The leaves also help heal bruises."

Chloë hardly listened. She was worried about the mushrooms. "You're not going to eat those," she said, pointing to the mushrooms.

"Yes I am."

"They're poisonous, you know. They're called toadstools. They make the blood behind your eyeballs curdle like milk gone sour, and you go blind. It's very painful, lethal and, I think, illegal."

Bernadette said, "I don't bother with the poisonous ones, and they don't bother with me."

"What about these pansies? They have faces. You said you don't eat anything that has a face."

"A literal interpretation is the last refuge of a small mind," she said. "You're being picky, Chloë. Picky, picky, picky."

"Is this why you were called a flower child?" Chloë asked. "I have to warn you, Nick has told me all about your life at Spinach Hill."

Bernadette replied, "Those days were a long time ago. Long ago. We were flower children," she said. "We called ourselves that, even though Nick was really the only child among us."

Chloë sat at the table, her hands folded in her lap and said, "I can't eat this, you know."

"Oh!" Bernadette said. "I think you can."

She sat at the table and watched as Bernadette ate. She kept her hands in her lap and would not lift a fork. If Bernadette was aware of being stared at, she gave no indication. She finished one bowl of salad and took another. Chloë buttered a roll and ate that. Bernadette finished her second bowl of salad and got up from the table. She took some coffee beans from the freezer and ground them in the small electric mill. She put the coffee grinds into a paper filter and set the kettle on the stove to boil.

While her back was turned, Chloë ventured to take a forkful of salad. It was not exactly what she was used to.

The dressing had a tart and yeasty flavor, and she found herself taking a second bite to figure out the mystery of the taste. Her third forkful was halfway to her mouth when Bernadette turned around to sit back down at the table and wait for the water to boil. Chloë was embarrassed to be caught eating what she had said she would not, but Bernadette acted as if Chloë's eating the salad was the most natural thing in the world. Chloë finished her one bowlful and took a second.

Bernadette asked Chloë if she would like to join her in the living room for a cup of coffee.

"Is that European?" Chloë asked. "Giving coffee to children and having it in the living room?"

Bernadette replied, "I don't know if it's European or not. It's what I like to do. You may join me if you like."

Chloë couldn't figure out if she liked the coffee itself or the ritual of drinking it in the living room after supper. But by the end of her first week there, it was no longer unexpected and was very welcome.

* * *

Besides learning to swim, Chloë also learned to play cribbage. She had never even shuffled a deck of cards, but before their first week was out, Bernadette had taught Chloë how to play cribbage, her favorite. Chloë loved keeping score by moving the little pegs along the board, and cribbage quickly became her favorite too.

When at last she won a game, she said, "I must have card sense."

Bernadette replied, "You must have a good teacher."

Chloë said, "Have you ever known any twelve-year-old who learned as fast as me?"

Bernadette replied, "Me."

* * *

On Friday of that first week the sky was overcast, and before they left the Ritz, Bernadette closed up the van and stood on a high dune, looking out on that huge volume of gray.

"Won't we go swimming today?" Chloë asked.

"Of course we will. Only sissies need sunshine to swim."

As they started back toward the van, Bernadette looked over her shoulder and said, "It's a funny thing about horizons. You can never get close to them, but you sure do miss them when they're not visible."

That afternoon when they arrived at Seminole Beach, Chloë raced from the car and plunged right in. It was riptide, and she got carried out by the current. Before she realized it, she was in water up to her neck. She ducked under and bobbed up again and found the dog at her side. Well, she thought, I've gotten as good as this animal. It wasn't until she turned to wave to Bernadette that she realized that her feet couldn't touch bottom.

She didn't panic. She knew she would be able to swim back. Maybe her form would not be Olympic class, but she knew she could face the unexpected all the way back to shore. And she did.

When she got back, she dried off and said to Bernadette, "I think I can save you now if I want to."

As she climbed the dune on her way to the car, Chloë allowed the soft drizzle from the sky and the salt spray from the ocean to wash over her. The sea and the sky and the sand had all become one, something that was neither water, air, nor land and yet was all three.

Over the course of that first week, Bernadette, Chloë, and Daisy had a start on becoming something that was neither woman, child, nor dog and yet was all three. Chloë no longer thought of Daisy as an animal. Daisy had become one. So had she. Chloë liked being *one* and *three-in-one* at the same time.

On their first Saturday—and the Saturdays that would follow—they did the laundry, cleaned the house, and shopped for groceries. Chloë quickly learned to cruise the aisles of the supermarket to search for food that did not look like anything they served in the van, did not taste like anything they served in the van and, most especially, did not smell anything like it either. They bought bushels of fruit and fresh vegetables and cartons of breakfast cereal.

And in the late afternoon, they again went to the beach. After Chloë's swimming lesson, Bernadette sat under a large umbrella and read.

On Sunday Bernadette washed her Firebird and worked under its hood. She took a stethoscope to the motor. "Checking its heart?" Chloë asked.

"The valves," Bernadette answered.

Bernadette finished her work on the car before noon, and in the late afternoon they went to the beach again, taking along a picnic supper this time.

On Chloë's second Saturday in Peco, it rained.

The summer rains of Peco are so particular that one side of a street can get soaked while the other side stays totally dry. And when the rain clears, it exits quickly, as if it is embarrassed. By the time they got home from grocery shopping, the rain had come and gone.

Bernadette rushed outside to see what the rain had done to her garden. After even so brief a rain, the earth of Peco gets steamy. Cement paths look moist enough to grow crops. Large bushes droop from the weight of water, and every color looks like the utmost shade of something natural. Bernadette pulled a few weeds from the flower beds and then wandered out to the field behind the house. "There will be a good selection of mushrooms tomorrow. There always is after a rain," she said, smiling. "I'll need them. We're having company for supper. Zack and Wanda are coming over."

Chloë's spirits sank.

Every time they ran into Zack at the commissary, he made a comment about "the kid," and every time he did, Bernadette said, "She's Nick's kid, Zack, and her name is Chloë." When she said that, Zack would smile a secret smile and continue on his rounds.

There was something going on between Zack and Bernadette that Chloë couldn't explain. Zack was not exactly teasing every time he insisted on saying *the kid*, and Bernadette was not exactly teasing every time she insisted upon correcting him. Nick's kid, she would say. Zack's smile—neither slow nor twitchy, but sly and secret—was one she couldn't explain. Did he know that she was not really Nick's kid? Or did he possibly think that Chloë herself didn't know that she was adopted?

There was something going on between Wanda and Zack that she could explain. Wanda was Zack's girlfriend. She had been working for Zack for a year and had been his girlfriend for one month less than that. She worked the highway route. The highway route was always the job for the newest employee.

Chloë was grateful that she had to see Zack only for short periods of time. Until now. Now she would have to spend a whole evening in his company. She was ready to protest, to tell Bernadette that she did enough food service during the week and deserved a day of rest and recreation, but something stopped her from complaining.

Something in her heart told her not to complain.

That something—which she recognized but could not describe—told her that Bernadette had invited Wanda and Zack over because she wanted them to see the *us* she and Bernadette had become.

Then, unexpectedly, Bernadette asked, "Would you like to go to a movie this afternoon?"

Chloë said yes.

Chloë loved movies. Anjelica and Krystal had probably seen every new release at least once since summer began. In Ridgewood, in order to fit in, it was important to keep up. But that was one part of fitting in that was easy for Chloë. Unlike going to slumber parties or the pet store at the mall, she loved going to the movies.

To Bernadette, movies did not mean the multiplex inside the mall. To Bernadette movies meant the dollar movie in a strip mall where all the stores except Karl's Sandwich Shop had moved out. Chloë looked over the list on the marquee; she had already seen every one; four were already out on video. If Bernadette gave her a choice, she wouldn't mind seeing *Father of the Bride* again.

A large section of the parking lot to the side and back of the movie was marked off with sawhorses and orange traffic cones. On their way to the box office, they wandered over to see what was going on. A bunch of kids were swooping around the back lot on Rollerblades, and in the section on the side, others were doing leaps and turns. Bernadette and Chloë stayed and watched so long, they missed the coming attractions.

Chloë hated missing the coming attractions. In Ridgewood she never did. And when the movie was over, she always stayed to see the credits—up to and including *best boy*—whatever that was. But *The End* was still flashing on the screen, and the music had not swelled to its full final crescendo before Bernadette was back out on the parking lot watching the skaters. Chloë followed, once again, feeling very much the grown-up.

All the beginners were gone. Only the spirited, the brave, and the athletically gifted remained. A man as old as Nick was practicing jumping over barriers. A pudgy woman was skating on one leg, and around the perimeter of the lot, a chain of seven men and women, hand-to-waist, were skating in wide circles at high speed.

Bernadette continued to watch the skaters, fascinated. "Looks like fun," she said, reluctantly pulling herself away and reaching into her pocket for her car keys.

Rollerblades were not new to Chloë. She had seen them before and thought of them as objects that created sweat and frizzy hair. In the almost two weeks she had spent in Peco, she had not conquered sweat but had conquered her fear of it. The frizzies were another matter. Whereas a good shower took care of the sweat, a good shampoo did not cure the frizzies. But Bernadette's life-style left her no time to fight it. Chloë washed her hair and let it dry in the air, certain that she was saving Bernadette millions of dollars worth of electricity because she was not using either a hair dryer or hot rollers. There were days when she did not recognize what she saw in the mirror, and other days when she didn't even bother to look.

7

On Sunday morning they waxed the car. With more direction from Bernadette than she felt was necessary, Chloë helped. After lunch they went together into the field behind the house and foraged for edible weeds and mushrooms. Bernadette washed all the salad ingredients and dried them in paper towels and arranged them in a huge, clear plastic bowl. It did look beautiful, and Chloë was honest when she said, "I don't know if we should eat it or take its picture."

Bernadette made a small curtsy and replied, "It is beautiful, isn't it?"

"It ain't bragging if it's true," Chloë said.

Bernadette stocked the refrigerator with beer and Coke and set out little bowls of trail mix and roasted peanuts. She said they would order in a pizza after everyone had settled down.

Everyone turned out to be a surprise. Wanda brought along her sister, Velma, and Velma brought along her son, Tyler.

Chloë had often seen Wanda at the commissary, but she had never seen as much of her as she saw that Sunday night. Wanda wore shorts and a halter top. The halter was cut low, and the shorts were cut high and low. High on the thigh, low on the waist. She wore a thin gold chain around her waist, where a belt should be, except the chain was so thin it couldn't hold anything up, even if there were something to. Wanda was a woman without wrinkles. No wrinkles. Even her belly button—an inny—looked unwrinkled.

She had let down her long blond hair.

Velma looked a lot like Wanda. Her hair was as long as Wanda's but was brown all the way past the roots. Her fingernails didn't stop; they were long enough to chop onions. Velma was two years younger than Wanda, every bit as unwrinkled as her sister and every inch as well-built. They were dressed like twins, only in different colors. Chloë thought they looked like two full-size Totally Hair Barbies—one blond, one brunette.

Besides dressing alike and looking alike, the sisters sounded alike. Not only did they have the same accent and the same way of saying things, they also had the same way of not saying things.

What Chloë sensed was that, for all the sisters showed of themselves, there was something underneath that they tried to hide.

There was no laughter beneath their smiles.

There was no heart beneath their cleavage.

Daisy was agitated. Bernadette called her into the kitchen and told her to sit.

Wanda said, "Chloë, darling, why don't you and Tyler take the dog for a walk."

Chloë said, "Daisy? Do you mean Daisy?"

Wanda smiled. "Yeah. Why don't you take it for a walk with Tyler."

"Daisy's a *she*," Chloë replied. "I would enjoy taking her and Tyler for a walk." She put on Daisy's leash and said, "Come along, Tyler. Come."

Tyler was thirteen. Chloë had often dreamed of what taking a walk with a teenaged boy would be like. This would be her first.

Chloë couldn't decide if Tyler didn't have the beginnings of facial hair or if it was too blond to show; his eyelashes were so blond, they looked invisible. He was slender and neat, and no taller than she was, even if he was a teenager. His hair was long for a boy's and as blond all the way to the roots as Wanda's was on the ends. He must have been a thumb-sucker long past the time his second teeth came in because he had an overbite that made his lips look like pages in a pop-up book that would not properly close. His voice was still soprano.

Taking Daisy along was a good idea. Holding the leash gave Chloë something to do with her hands, and having a well-trained animal gave her the feeling of being in control of something—even if it was only an animal that she had had no part in training.

They walked in silence for a few minutes before Chloë asked Tyler if he would be helping out on his aunt's van the way she helped out on Bernadette's. Tyler said, "No way. I'm enrolled in Bible school at the Church of the Endless Horizon. I already got started."

"Ah!" Chloë said. "The Church of the Endless Horizon. Endless horizon," she repeated dreamily. "It's a funny thing about horizons, Tyler. You can never get close to them, but you sure do miss them when they're not visible." She trusted that Bernadette wouldn't mind her cribbing. They walked a little bit farther. "With a name like that, your Bible school must be a wonderful place," she added, not believing it for a minute.

Tyler said, "Yeah, well, it's okay. I was at skating camp last summer. Tomorrow, I'm going Rollerblading. There's no sidewalks where Aunt Wanda lives, so I have to do it on the road when I get home from school. Can't hardly even practice, even though I'm already real good at it. Aunt Wanda promises that she's gonna find me a place. I was at swimming camp the year before and at nature camp the year before that. I know every kind of poisonous snake in these United States, and I touched two of them."

Chloë could have told Tyler about the parking lot at the dollar movie where he could practice his Rollerblading, but she didn't. "Can you skate backwards?" she asked.

"Nothing to it. Can swim backwards too. It's called the backstroke," Tyler replied.

"Bernadette taught me how to swim without ever doing it herself. She knows exactly what to do and how to teach it without even letting her feet off the ground. Learning from her is better than swimming camp."

Tyler shrugged. "I don't know about that. I just know I got real talent for learning stuff."

As they walked deeper into the field behind the house, Chloë hoped Daisy would show off how she found wild mushrooms. That was pretty impressive.

Like magic, Daisy did. She stopped dead in her tracks, her nose, back, and tail making a line so straight you could set bowling pins on it.

Chloë reached down to pick up the mushroom, and

Tyler yelled, "Don't touch it. Field mushrooms is poisonous. I learned all about them at nature camp."

"Wait until you taste the salad we made for supper."

"Do you mean she put them wild things into the salad we're supposed to eat tonight?"

"They're delicious."

"Oh, sure," Tyler said. "They may be delicious to you, but there's an old saying, *One man's meat is another man's poison.*"

"If you really had a talent for learning stuff, then you would know that they are not all poisonous. Bernadette knows which are and which are not." They walked in silence for a while, then Tyler began falling a few steps behind, acting as if he didn't want to walk with her. Chloë grew uncomfortable, then annoyed. He would walk with her. She would make him. She stopped dead in her tracks, Daisy by her side, and waited for him to catch up. He did, but he kept his hands in his pockets and his eyes down on the ground.

She said, "I chose to spend my summer in Peco because living with Bernadette is better than nature camp. It's like living with Mother Nature herself. She knows all about mushrooms and can make tea out of weeds and roots, and she does all the work on her Firebird herself. All of it. She spends most of her spare time under its hood."

Tyler's head jerked up, and his eyes opened wide. "What color is it?"

"Black with licks of flame on its hood."

"She has a hood?" he asked.

Chloë replied. "Of course. I just told you she spends a lot of time under the hood. That Firebird is so familiar, she knows it blindfolded."

Tyler said, "Well, the hoods is mostly how they get blindfolded."

Chloë was puzzled, but she wasn't about to let Tyler know that. "Bernadette told me that she had bought one of the first Tercels that came into this country, but it wasn't powerful enough for her, so she traded it in for an old Firebird."

Tyler said, "It's a well-known fact that male falcons is smaller, but they are powerful, too. But probably not as powerful as a Firebird."

Chloë said, "Bernadette never had a Falcon. Why would she want a Falcon when she has a Firebird?"

"A tercel is a falcon. It's male. I guess, being a female, your auntie would find the female more familiar, if you get my meaning."

Chloë did not get his meaning. As a matter of fact, she had no idea what he was talking about.

They had not walked much farther when the mushroom she was holding began to stain her hand. She started to throw it away. Tyler said, "Take a bite of it. I dare you."

"Are you crazy? I can't take a bite of it unless Bernadette okays it."

"I thought so," Tyler said. "That aunt of yours has you spooked, don't she?"

Chloë tilted her head back, looked at him out of half-lowered eyes, flared her nostrils, slowly opened her fingers, and allowed the mushroom to drop from her hand.

* * *

When they returned to the house, Velma asked Tyler if he had had a nice walk, and Tyler nodded yes without taking his eyes off Bernadette. He squinched up his eyes as if to concentrate and seemed unable to look at anyone else.

They had been back only a short time when Zack made an announcement that got everybody's attention.

"Marie's quitting," he said.

Marie worked Talleyrand, the same as Bernadette, but she didn't get the good spot.

"Who's going to take her place?" Bernadette asked.

Wanda said, "I am. Velma here is taking over my highway route."

Daisy chose that very minute to get up, walk over to Velma, and growl. That deep-in-the-throat, quiet-but-threatening growl that was her specialty. Bernadette allowed Daisy to get in a few good ones before calling her back. Tyler moved from the chair to the sofa beside his mother as if to protect her.

Wanda said, "I swear, Bernadette, that dog of yours is bewitched."

This time Tyler deliberately looked at Chloë and nodded ever so slightly. She didn't understand, so she returned his look through half-lowered eyes and flared her nostrils again.

* * *

It was time for pizza.

Bernadette asked what everyone wanted and then called in the wrong order. Chloë thought, A person who can remember which welder takes Sweet'n Low and which takes sugar and how many, can surely remember who wants pepperoni and who wants peppers. That is unless that person is upset. Daisy had known before anyone else. That was why she had growled at Velma.

* * *

Their guests went home immediately after eating, and Bernadette and Chloë were left with the mess. Working for Zack during the week was bad enough, but having to clean up after him on Sunday was the worst.

Bad as Zack was, Tyler was even worse. He was so sure of himself. He was too smug by half. Chloë felt as grouchy as she did when she came home from a slumber party. Bernadette looked up from wiping the table, and without either saying a word, Chloë knew that Bernadette was feeling every bit as grouchy as she was, and they finished cleaning up the kitchen in silence.

Bernadette said good-night and went to her room. Daisy followed.

What had happened? When the party had started, they had both felt like one and three-in-one. When the party was over, they didn't feel like it at all. Zack and Wanda, Tyler and Velma had not been company. They had been an invasion.

8

Chloë went to her room and took out her stationery. If ever there was a time to write to Anjelica and Krystal, this was it. She would write one letter addressed to both of them and tell them about the blond teenaged boy she had met. It would be easy to leave out the buckteeth, the bad grammar, and the parts of the conversation she didn't like. She thought about the crazy parts of the conversation that she had had with him and decided not to write a letter after all.

Instead she wrote a list.

She wrote a list of words: *falcon, tercel, familiar, hood.* Then she went into the living room, where Bernadette had her bookshelves, and she looked up each one of those words.

She had suspected that she and Tyler had not been talking about the same things, but it was not until she had looked everything up that she fully understood that *falcons, tercels, hoods,* and *familiar* meant one thing to him and something entirely different to her.

She had been talking about cars and auto mechanics.

He had been talking about birds and witchcraft.

To people in Ridgewood, a Falcon is an automobile manufactured by Ford, and a Tercel is an automobile manufactured by Toyota. Bernadette had once owned a Tercel, which she had traded in for her Firebird. It was the engine under the brightly painted metal hood of her Firebird that Bernadette knew very well; that was what Bernadette was *familiar* with.

To Tyler a tercel (spelled with a small *t*) was a male falcon, a kind of hawk, that people train to kill prey. Trained falcons (small *f*) wear a *hood* to blindfold them when they are not hunting.

To Tyler a *familiar* meant a witch's spirit that took an animal form. Birds and dogs were often thought to be witches' familiars.

Once again Chloë went over her conversation with Tyler. *Tyler was worried about Bernadette's being a witch.* What a joke it would be to convince him that she was. She almost laughed out loud. It would be easy. She remembered the small thrill of satisfaction she had felt as she had watched Tyler edge closer to his mother when Daisy had growled at her. She would multiply that feeling a hundred times by watching him squirm as—little by little—she convinced him that Bernadette was a witch, and that she, Chloë, was learning her powers. It would be fun.

And it would be easy. For one thing, there was a lot about Bernadette that was mysterious. The way she didn't allow anyone in her room after she went to bed. The way she never went swimming even though she knew how. The way she knew all about wild food. The way she made

Daisy so obedient. Tyler had said, "That aunt of yours has you spooked, doesn't she?" He was halfway to believing already.

Chloë smiled to herself. At this very moment, he was probably wondering whether Daisy or the Firebird was Bernadette's familiar. Once he found out that the Firebird was a car and could not be a familiar, it would be easy to convince him that Daisy was. After all, there was a lot about Daisy that was mysterious. The animal did seem to have a sixth sense about things. Look at the way she had growled at Velma. Daisy would help her convince Tyler.

Chloë took notes on everything she looked up. She returned the encyclopedias to the shelf under the window seat and thought, How amusing it will be to teach this beardless wonder who was so good at "learning stuff." He won't be so smug when he learns that he has been made a fool. So he had touched two poisonous snakes. So what! So he could swim. So what! So he could swim backwards and Rollerblade. He's just "got a real talent for learning stuff." So what!

That's when the idea hit her. She knew what she would do with the fifty dollars. She would buy two pairs of Rollerblades. A set for Bernadette, and a set for her. She would learn how to Rollerblade and then invite Tyler to the dollar-movie parking lot. She was glad she had not told him about it.

The more she thought about buying Rollerblades, the more she liked the idea. Rollerblades would make the perfect hospitality present. She wished she could go to a store, buy the skates, and surprise Bernadette, but there was nothing within walking distance of the house except the field where the mushrooms grew.

Since she couldn't surprise Bernadette with the skates themselves, she decided to compose a gift certificate and surprise her with that.

Chloë took a fresh sheet of stationery and made up a gift certificate. She used a book for a straight-edge and printed everything in her best letters, signed her full name in cursive, even though using all four of her names caused her to almost run out of space. She drew a decorative border around the edge. Having black ink made it look very professional. As a matter of fact, she thought her certificate was suitable for framing. It took over an hour to finish, but having it take so long made it seem even more worthwhile.

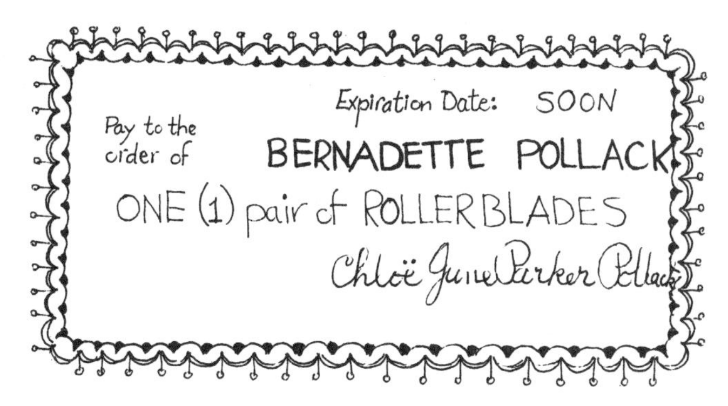

She wished she could present it to Bernadette right away, but she knew that this was hardly an emergency, and she had been reminded every night that once Bernadette had gone into her bedroom and closed the door, she was not to be disturbed. She could slip it under the bedroom door, but she wanted to see Bernadette's face when she got it, so she took it into the kitchen. She thought of putting it on the refrigerator door with a magnet, but she didn't want to cover up even the tiniest corner of her work, so she propped it up by the Cuisinart.

She returned to her room and tucked the pages of research notes under the lining of the top drawer of her dresser.

She lay between the clean, crisp sheets and decided that she could deal with Tyler. From not caring if she never saw him again, she couldn't wait for their next meeting.

Chloë jumped out of bed the minute she heard footsteps in the hall. She ran into the kitchen, retrieved the gift certificate, and intercepted Bernadette on her way to the bathroom.

Bernadette had to go back to her bedroom to get her glasses before she could read it, but she looked pleased, really pleased, when she did. "I see I have to cash this in soon," she said. "We'll stop at the store right after work."

* * *

Velma was trouble from the get-go. That first morning she and Wanda came to work together, they each wore jeans that fit as tight as cuticle and that Chloë knew from experience would be hot to work in. The shirts they wore were cool: tight but sleeveless. On a man you would call them muscle shirts but on Wanda/Velma, it wasn't muscle that showed. The women drivers—except for Bernadette—stared as hard as the men. Zack stared and came out of his office three times that morning. He laughed and thwacked his leg and rolled his eyes and said that he was doing his part to keep Florida beautiful.

Talleyrand was busy that first day that Wanda took over for Marie, so by the time they drove out to the Ritz, Chloë was hot and tired and anxious to finish up so that they could buy their Rollerblades.

When Bernadette pulled up to the Ritz, one of Zack's vans was already there, parked where the bulldozers were digging the pool. "Chloë," Bernadette said, "we have trouble, and its name starts with a *T*."

Chloë stuck her head out the window as they circled the site, but she couldn't see the driver. As soon as Bernadette stopped, Chloë hopped down from the van and started toward the workers, who were standing three and four deep, lifting their arms over the crowd, either to give the driver money or take supplies from her. There was so much laughing and jostling going on, no one even noticed that Chloë had wormed her way to the center of the half-circle that fanned out from the van.

There was Velma.

Velma did not notice Chloë. She was laughing and reaching a hot dog high over her head. She was wearing a bathing suit that covered as little as it left to the imagination.

When Chloë returned to the van, she said, "It starts with a *V*, not a *T*. It's Velma."

Bernadette asked, "What was she wearing?"

Chloë replied, "Almost nothing."

Bernadette said, "That *almost nothing* is called a T-back."

Chloë said, "I didn't think real people wore them. I had only seen them in magazines or on calendars before."

Bernadette said, "I expected it. The minute she walked through the door of my house, I knew that my life would change. When Zack announced that Marie was quitting, I felt a sudden chill go through me."

Chloë said, "Daisy felt it too. Remember how she acted? You had to call her into the kitchen and tell her to sit."

Bernadette nodded. "When I went to bed, I lay there thinking about Velma, and I knew what she was going to do. I knew she would wear a T-back. And this is only the start."

She backed the van out to the road. They never found out if Velma noticed that they had been there. They knew the workmen hadn't.

On the way to the commissary, Chloë asked herself, How many women could predict that someone would wear a T-back? And how many dogs could read minds as well as mushrooms? They were going to make it very easy to convince Tyler that Bernadette was a witch and that Daisy was her familiar. Chloë could hardly wait to get good on Rollerblades, so she could make a date with Tyler.

10

They went to two sporting-goods stores, one very large toy store, and a Walmart. Comparison shopping proved that fifty dollars hardly paid for a single pair of Rollerblades.

Bernadette reached into her pocketbook and took out a check. It was made out to Chloë. "Your paycheck," she said. "I forgot to give it to you."

"Is this minimum wage?" Chloë asked.

"You betcha," Bernadette answered and checked her watch. "We have time to stop at the bank and cash it if you want. Do you know how to endorse a check?"

Chloë said that she knew how to use a credit card and didn't think endorsing a paycheck—even if it was her first—could be any more difficult.

It was necessary to go to the bank where Bernadette had her account so that she could verify Chloë's signature. They returned to the sporting-goods store and bought what the clerk called "in-line" skates. He tried to talk them into buying wrist and elbow guards, knee pads and helmets, but Chloë was firm. She would not buy them. She told him that she was a minimum-wage earner and didn't have money for extras. Furthermore, she did not believe that beginners needed to have all that equipment weighing them down.

The clerk said that beginners especially needed the extras for protection, but Chloë wouldn't buy either his argument or his equipment. When he went back into the stockroom, she told Bernadette that he was probably working on commission and would try to sell them anything just to raise his sales volume. "That's what it means to get paid commission," Chloë said, "the more money you take in, the more money you make."

Bernadette said, "Fancy that. You don't suppose that that is in any way related to the way I do business, do you?"

Chloë only meant to show Bernadette that she was an experienced consumer and that all those trips to the mall with Anjelica and Krystal had taught her something. "You told me that the customer is always right. Right here, right now, we are the customers, and we're not buying any extras."

* * *

Rollerblading looked easy but wasn't. It was closer to ice-skating than it was to roller-skating. A person's ankles can turn in on Rollerblades as easily as they can on ice skates. The lot was larger than it appeared to be when they'd been watching from the sidelines. Twice around and a beginner's ankles can hurt a lot.

Chloë knew she was getting a blister on the outside edge of her big toe. Not that she had ever before had a blister there, but she knew this was a big one. Probably huge. Probably on both big toes. Forget the sweat. Forget the frizzies. All she could think about was pain. She was experiencing major pain. She made it over to the curb and sat down.

She searched for Bernadette all over the beginners' side and couldn't find her. She stood up and scanned the crowd on the advanced side. There was Bernadette. Skating backwards! Having a wonderful time. It was not fair that someone who was forty-five years old could be that good that fast.

Chloë sat down again and buried her head in her hands. She had to rethink Rollerblading. She was not asking to be athletically gifted. She had hoped that Rollerblading would give her a chance to have another encounter with Tyler, but now she would settle for a little gain without pain. She closed her eyes and tried not to think about her toes and wished as hard as she did when she blew out her birthday candles that Bernadette would stop. *Stop.*

It was getting dark. They hadn't turned on the lights in the parking lot yet. Peco had almost no twilight. The light can be good one minute and bad the next, and when Chloë next looked up, it seemed to her that night as dark as her thoughts had descended. She stood up, spotted Bernadette, and frantically waved. She finally caught her eye, and Bernadette started skating toward her.

Her wishes were about to be answered.

In the dusk it was hard to tell where the curb ended and its shadow began.

Bernadette tripped.

As she fell forward, she threw her arms out in front of her to break her fall. It was the worst thing she could do.

Other skaters who were nearby helped her up.

Chloë whipped across the parking lot and got to Bernadette just as they helped her into the Firebird. Bernadette sat in the driver's seat with her feet sticking out the door. Her knees were skinned, but it was her wrist that was hurting. It was already beginning to swell. One of the skaters asked Bernadette if she could drive.

"It's my left wrist," she said. "I hardly need it for driving." Her mouth was so dry, her upper lip stuck on her teeth as she spoke. Once she was behind the wheel, she said, "We have to make a stop at the hospital emergency room."

"Is it broken?" Chloë asked.

"How am I supposed to know? Isn't that what X rays are for?"

"Are you hurting real bad, Bernadette?"

"Not as bad as you're going to hurt if you ask one more dumb question."

* * *

When they got to the hospital, Bernadette asked Chloë to fill out the forms for her. There were enough questions to fill volume *Garrison–Halibut* of the *Encyclopaedia Britannica.* Chloë copied Bernadette's social security number from a card she found in her wallet and consulted with Bernadette about allergies and childhood diseases before checking the boxes on the forms.

Bernadette closed her eyes and rested her head against the emergency-room wall. "Any life-threatening illnesses?" Chloë asked.

"Not at the moment," Bernadette said, "but if they don't get here soon, I may threaten a few lives myself."

Chloë began to write and then asked, "How do you spell *penumbra*?"

Bernadette answered, "P-E-N-U-M-B-R-A."

"That's what I thought," Chloë said. She wrote a while longer and then asked, "Is *gratuitous* spelled with an *i* before the *o-u-s*? It means unnecessary."

Bernadette said, "I know what it means. G-R-A-T-U . . ." and then she yelled, "What are you doing?"

"They asked for a description of the accident."

Bernadette said, "You don't have to try for a Pulitzer Prize, Chloë. Just give them the facts."

"Those are the facts. If the light had been good, there would have been no penumbra, and you wouldn't have fallen gratuitously."

Bernadette closed her eyes and leaned back against the wall. She held her injured wrist with her healthy hand. Without opening her eyes, she said, "It wasn't your fault, Chloë, no matter what you were wishing."

She knew! Bernadette knew. She had known from the minute the accident happened what Chloë had been wishing for.

Chloë finished a thorough and poetic description of the accident before the nurse came to interview Bernadette. By the time they were ready to take X rays, Bernadette's wrist and hand were so swollen they looked like a cow's udder with five dangles instead of four.

X rays showed a hairline fracture of one of the bones of her wrist. A medical assistant put it in a cast. The doctor offered Bernadette a pain pill, but she didn't want to drive under the influence of a pill that could possibly make her sleepy, so she put it into her shirt pocket to take when she got home. The doctor also gave her medicine that was supposed to bring down the swelling, as well as a prescription for more pain pills.

She and Chloë stopped at a drugstore to fill the prescription, and by the time they got to the house, Daisy was pawing the floor, whimpering, circling, doing all the things that Daisy did when she was not at peace or had to relieve herself very badly. Once they were inside, Daisy jumped up on Bernadette. Instead of trying to lick her face as she usually did, Daisy tried to climb inside Bernadette's shirt pocket.

"Down, Daisy. Down," Bernadette said, but Daisy wouldn't get down. As tired and as hurting as Bernadette was, she took time to calm Daisy. She took the pain pill out of her pocket and the medicine from the bag and let Daisy get a good whiff of them. "Good dog," she said. Chloë watched, mystified. "Daisy can't forget that she was a drug-sniffing police dog," Bernadette explained. "She got a whiff of my pocket and did her duty."

Chloë brought Bernadette a glass of water so that she could swallow the pills. Bernadette asked Chloë if she would mind taking Daisy for a run around the block to let her work off some energy. "When you get back, I'll tell you how I got Daisy," she said.

Daisy had been trained by the Canine Corps to be a drug-sniffing dog. She had lived with Jake, her handler. He brought her to the docks when the stevedores were unloading cargo from overseas. Jake was a cop. Daisy was his second drug-sniffing dog. The first one had been killed in a shoot-out at a drug arrest in town. Jake had had Daisy only a year and a half when he suffered a heart attack right in the warehouse where he and Daisy had been inspecting cargo from Venezuela.

When Jake fell, Daisy set up a howl that made everyone come running. But Daisy wouldn't let anyone near her master. Drug-sniffing dogs are trained to take orders only from their masters, so Daisy snarled and snapped, and it was worth a person's life to try to get close enough to Jake to give him CPR.

Bernadette heard the commotion and ran into the warehouse. She saw Daisy sitting beside her fallen master and a circle of people standing five feet away. Jake and Daisy looked like the bulls-eye on a target.

Bernadette didn't charge into the circle. She crouched at the edge and whispered to the man next to her, "Call 911." Then she whispered again—this time, no one—not even those standing right next to her—could understand what she was whispering. They could hardly hear her. But Daisy must have, for she lay down, put her head between her paws and allowed Bernadette to approach. Bernadette didn't walk upright and she didn't make any sudden moves. She crawled to Jake. Crawled on all fours. Daisy moved nothing but her eyes, yet under her sleek black coat, every muscle appeared outlined and ready.

Bernadette knew that Rule 1 in CPR was, Try

to wake the victim. *Shake and shout* was the first order of business. But Bernadette knew that she would have Daisy's teeth at her throat if she shook Jake. Slowly, slowly, slowly she lowered her head to Jake's chest to listen for a heartbeat. There was none. She felt for a pulse in his neck. There was none. Slowly, slowly, slowly she tilted his head back, pried open his mouth, and gave him the kiss of life. But Jake did not respond. Daisy watched Bernadette without moving her head, her eyes riveted on Bernadette like a New Zealand heading dog.

Bernadette worked on Jake for a full ten minutes before she gave up. She folded Jake's hands over his chest and turned his face toward Daisy. Daisy stood up, went over to Jake, licked his face, stopped, licked his face again, then sat at his side, lifted her head, and howled. She howled so loud, you could see the waves of sound as they rose in her throat.

Bernadette did not try to comfort Daisy. She let her howl. She got up slowly and stood over Jake's body.

No one moved until the rescue squad arrived and broke through the circle. Bernadette took Daisy's leash and led her out to her van. Dogs from the Canine Corps don't usually bond with anyone besides their handlers, and it can be dan-

> gerous for anyone else to try. Sometimes they are so hostile to anyone besides their handlers, they have to be put down, but Daisy and Bernadette got together the day that Jake died. They have been together ever since.

Bernadette's eyelids were getting heavy. She needed sleep. At that moment, Chloë was so proud of Bernadette, so full of admiration, she could hardly talk. Yet, even as Bernadette was telling the story, she was thinking how it fit right in with what she wanted to tell Tyler.

11

The following morning, Chloë awakened before Bernadette called her. She started to turn over, to wait for her call, but she sensed by the slant of the light in the room that it was late. She jumped out of bed and ran into the kitchen to look at the clock. It was 6:45. Six-forty-five! Fifteen minutes past the time they should have been at Zack's!

This was an emergency.

She ran toward Bernadette's bedroom, ready to pound on the door to break the news to her. She had never once disturbed Bernadette from the time she entered her bedroom at night until she was called in the morning. But this definitely was an emergency. She lifted her hand to knock on the door but didn't. She suddenly felt very shy about invading Bernadette's privacy.

Instead of knocking on the door to awaken her, she opened the door slowly. The first thing she saw was Daisy on the floor at the foot of the bed. Daisy's head turned, and Chloë signaled her to stay quiet. She looked around the room. The Florida sun pressed through the blinds, giving it an apricot glow. Chloë had never before seen Bernadette asleep. She was lying on her side, her back to the door, her good arm curved under the pillow, her injured arm lying on top of it, making a heavy dent. Chloë focused on the naked shoulder that was visible above the blanket. She felt embarrassed being there.

She hesitated.

This truly was an emergency.

She had to do something.

In a flash she knew what she would do. She would both welcome the unexpected and help Bernadette. She beckoned to Daisy to come and quietly closed Bernadette's door behind her. She led her through the kitchen door and shooed her outside to do her business. "Be quick about it," she said.

She checked the list of numbers that Bernadette had posted by the phone. She found Grady Oates. She dialed. As the phone rang—once, twice, three times—she waited for a muffled click and the dread sound of low static that would tell her that she was about to speak to an answering machine. *Please, Grady, please answer. Please, please, please. Please, no answering machine. Please. Please. Please be there.*

After the fifth ring, she heard Grady's deep, warm voice say, "Hello." She quickly explained what had happened and asked him if, instead of going to the commissary, he would please come pick her up. "Will you please drive Bernadette's van today? I'll help," she said. "I know the routine, and I am very good with condiments. Then I'll help you with your job at the mall. I promise I will."

* * *

Chloë and Grady were so late getting to the commissary that there were no ham or tuna sandwiches left. They loaded up as best they could and headed out to Talleyrand. There was no chance of their getting the best spot. They were the last van in line at Talleyrand. As soon as Grady parked, Chloë hopped out, opened the window, put up the awning, and set out the condiments. No one came. The only van doing business—and it was doing excellent business—was the one in Bernadette's old spot.

Chloë went down the line to see what was going on and asked Grady to please wait by the van to catch any stray business that might come their way.

Down the line she went. One van, two vans, three vans, four. Down the line, at van number five, in the spot that used to be Bernadette's, there was a battalion of men, their arms raised to the sky in an effort to give money or receive goods from driver-server Wanda. *Ditto to yesterday.*

Wanda was busy. Very busy. She was wearing a T-back. *Ditto to yesterday.*

On the other side of the crowd, two of the vans were serving a couple of women who worked in the shipyards. The others were doing zero business. Nothing. *Nada.* Zilch.

Chloë returned to Grady. "It wouldn't have made any difference if we had gotten the best spot," she said. "It wouldn't have made any difference at all." Chloë told him what was happening down the road and what had happened yesterday at the Ritz.

Grady burst out laughing. "There's an old saying in business," he said. "*Don't sell the steak, sell the sizzle.* Wanda and Velma are selling sizzle."

They managed to do some business with the shopworkers, but they were at a disadvantage because they didn't have ham or tuna sandwiches, both popular summertime items. When it was time to swing back to the docks to take care of lunch hour there, they could have been selling panty hose in a monastery for all the customers they had.

* * *

When they returned to the commissary, they saw Bernadette's Firebird in the parking lot. She was inside talking to Zack. "Out partying all night?" he asked, smiling. Bernadette didn't answer. "Seeing someone special for a late-late show?" he asked.

Bernadette said, "The only thing worse than a smart-mouthed man who is not witty is a smart-mouthed man who thinks he is."

Zack laughed, and winked at Grady and Chloë as they approached. Bernadette saw them and lifted her arm to wave. That was when Zack noticed the cast on her arm. "What happened to you?" he asked. "Did you have an accident? I didn't notice. I'm sorry. You know what a madhouse it is around here in the morning. What happened?" he asked.

"If you're not interested in finding out why, once in seven years, I am late for work, I'm not interested in giving you an education," Bernadette said. She turned her back and walked away.

Grady and Chloë unloaded Bernadette's van. Bernadette did what she could to help and signed the clipboard that Zack silently held out to her. Then they walked with Grady to his van. Once he was behind the wheel, Bernadette leaned against the window on the driver's side and said, "I owe you, Grady. I don't forget favors."

"Neither do I, Bernadette. I remember who got me this job in the first place." He put the key in the ignition. "Funny thing. I was on my way out the door when the phone rang, and I almost didn't answer, but the Lord turned me around and led me back to the phone. I tell you, Bernadette, I was only too happy to have your niece call on me. Delighted, I say."

"We're in for some changes, Grady," Bernadette said.

"Oh!" Grady replied, laughing. "I've already seen the sizzle." He waved good-bye.

* * *

By Wednesday, four out of seven of the women driver-servers on Talleyrand wore T-backs. Wanda and three others.

Thursday: Josetta and Lenore showed up in them. Josetta and Lenore were very large women. Chloë told Bernadette that they must have bought their T-backs from a Sumo-wrestler supply house.

Bernadette said, "Oh! I don't know. If God had wanted us all to be thin and firm, He wouldn't have given us a taste for cheese and chocolate."

Friday: Lionel, the one male driver-server on Talleyrand, showed up in a T-back. Lionel said, "Equal's equal, and fair's fair." The women shoved folded paper money into the strap of Lionel's T-back, and didn't ask for change. Chloë noticed that the men were not shoving dollar bills into the straps of the women's T-backs. She thought, if *equal* were really *equal*, they would.

Bernadette's sales were way down, and since Velma had usurped their place at the Ritz, they were returning to the commissary with most of what they had loaded.

* * *

On the second Friday of T-backs, Zack told Bernadette that he would like to see her in his office.

Chloë followed. Zack stopped in his tracks. "It's Bernadette I want to talk to."

"Chloë can come," Bernadette said.

Bernadette and Chloë sat down. Zack asked if they would like something cold to drink. Both refused. He cleared his throat several times, and at last said, "I don't know what's happening, Bernadette. You used to be my best driver-server." He picked up her clipboard and flipped through the week's receipts. "Your sales are way down. Way, way down." He asked if having the kid along was keeping her from giving her customers the kind of service she used to, and Bernadette said, "Chloë's a big help, Zack." He asked if something else was keeping her from giving her customers the kind of service she used to, and Bernadette said, "Maybe." Then he asked Bernadette if she thought she needed a change. She asked what kind of change.

"Time off. A little vacation maybe. Time to spend with the kid."

She said, "No, thank you."

Zack cleared his throat so that he could start a new paragraph. "I've been thinking about giving Velma the Talleyrand route and shifting you to the highway. For your own good, Bernadette. It might be a little less wear and tear on you. Velma's brought that highway route right along. She's bringing in almost as much business from that stop as we do on Talleyrand." Zack started reaching for another clipboard. "Here," he said, "I'll show you."

"You don't have to, Zack. I believe you."

"So you'll take Velma's route, then?" he asked.

"Sure," Bernadette said.

Chloë asked, "If Velma's doing so terrifically well out there on the highway, why pull her off?"

"Because I said that it will be easier on your aunt."

"Do you know wha—," Chloë started to say, but Bernadette interrupted her.

"When do I start?"

He got busy with some papers on his desk. "Monday," he said.

Zack never mentioned T-backs because, up to this point, work at the commissary had gone on as if they did not exist. Everyone who wore a T-back on the job continued to wear jeans and shirts over them at the commissary, both when they loaded up in the morning and when they checked in at night. The syllables *T-back* never crossed anyone's lips, and the outfits themselves never seemed to cross the threshold.

So by the end of the first full week of T-backs, so after being with Zack for seven years, after years of building up business, Bernadette lost Talleyrand. The progress that she had measured in years, Wanda measured in months, and Velma, days.

Bernadette and Chloë settled into a new work routine.

Chloë said, "I won't take any more salary, Bernadette, until we've gotten our commissions back up to what they were on Talleyrand."

Bernadette said, "Thank you. I've never had much trouble living within my means. I always make sure that my wants don't exceed my needs by too much. I thank you for your offer, Chlöe, and I accept."

Bernadette's accepting Chloë's offer meant that she took her help seriously, and that made Chloë feel even more helpful.

Within a week of driving the highway route, they began servicing the construction sites of a large office park south of town and the condos at Crossroads. Work was not easier than it was on Talleyrand because they had to hustle from place to place, but Bernadette had known it wouldn't be. And she knew that Zack knew it too.

Once their new routine was established, they returned to the sporting-goods store and bought wrist guards, elbow guards, and knee pads, taking great pains to avoid the clerk who had waited on them the first time. Neither Chloë nor Bernadette wanted to give him the satisfaction of seeing Bernadette's wrist in a cast.

Chloë learned to keep her ankles straight and to skate backwards. She was not doing spins or camels, but she figured when you start at square one, all improvement is one hundred percent.

She had thought about Tyler a lot, so on the day that Bernadette was due for a checkup on her arm, Chloë invited him to join her at the dollar-movie parking lot. Bernadette arranged to pick him up on her way to the doctor's office.

While waiting for Bernadette to shower, Chloë flipped on the TV to watch the early news. The weather report was the only part she was interested in. Heavy rains meant that there would be no work on the highway, and the condo and the office-park construction would be cut by half.

Just before the first commercial break, the male anchorperson said, "How much will the traffic on Talleyrand bear? That story and more as the news continues." Chloë turned up the volume and called Bernadette. "Something's happened on Talleyrand." Bernadette came running, and they turned their full attention to NewsCenter Five.

There was a little news and a sports report, followed by laughter, chitchat, and a few commercial messages. A little more news and the weather report, followed by laughter, chitchat, and a few commercial messages.

Chloë lost patience. "I can't figure out why they need two anchorpersons in the first place," she said. "They take up half the time talking to each other, and there's so little news, they have to divvy up the sentences between them. How come the networks need only one anchorperson for news of the whole U.S.A.?"

Bernadette just shrugged. "When you figure it out, tell me."

* * *

A tape of the first news broadcast about the T-backs showed the following:

> ANCHOR I: NewsCenter Five reporter Richard Roebuck went down to the docks on Talleyrand earlier this afternoon and has filed this report. Richard?
>
> RICHARD ROEBUCK (*close up, holding a microphone*): There is something old and something new on Talleyrand today. (*The camera pans to a line of driver-servers, their backs to the camera. Blue blobs cover their lower halves.*) Answering a call from a disgruntled employee, we went to Talleyrand today to find shipyard workers enjoying an old service with a new twist. (*The camera continues to pan up and down the line of servers as Richard Roebuck's voice explains the new dress code on Talleyrand.*) We spoke to several of the T-back wearers today.
>
> WANDA (*Only her head and neck are in view. She moistens her lips, smiles into the camera.*):

Wearing a T-back is a form of self-expression. (*The camera pans over the row of blue-blobs. Velma, her head turned so far around that the veins in her neck look like the coils of a spiral notebook, comes into sharp focus. Her smile is as wide as a porpoise's. She moistens her lips twice before the camera moves on.*)

RICHARD ROEBUCK: Self-expression? The disgruntled employee who called us did not call it that. Whatever you say it is, you have to admit that business on Talleyrand . . . is . . . booming.

ANCHOR I (*fighting back a smile*): Have they broken any laws?

ROEBUCK: None that we could find. The city has no ordinance banning T-backs or, as some people call them, *thongs*.

ANCHOR II: Thank you, Richard. Florida's most endangered species has a new friend. That and more coming up after these commercial messages.

ANCHORS I AND II shuffle papers, smile at each other.

Chloë turned off the TV. "Who do you think was the disgruntled employee?"

"Probably Wanda," Bernadette replied.

Chloë said, "I thought that *disgruntled* meant that the employee was unhappy with the situation."

Bernadette smiled. "Depends on the situation."

* * *

Wanda lived in a house that was a twin of Bernadette's, except that it was as far west of Talleyrand as Bernadette's was south of it. Tyler waited in the carport. He wore bicycle pants, knee pads, and wrist and elbow braces. His blades were tied together over his shoulder. He looked professional. Chloë's heart sank.

Wanda and Velma were also in the carport. Bernadette asked them about their appearance on the local news. Velma bragged about how Wanda had called the television station to tell them that there might be a story on Talleyrand if they got a reporter there at 10 A.M.

Chloë asked, "How come the reporter said that they answered a call from a disgruntled employee?"

Wanda laughed. "Honey, so little attention was being paid to the revolution down there on Talleyrand, that me and Velma *was* disgruntled, weren't we, Velma?"

Chloë said, "Bernadette guessed it was you." She started to say something else, but Bernadette flashed her a look that silenced her.

Velma said, "Well, you know how they are always asking people to dial *star-five* and phone in fast-breaking news stories. Well, Wanda figured we was worth five stars."

Wanda bragged, "They asked me if they should send an investigative reporter or just a field man, and I said, 'Honey, just send the straightest talker with the best eyesight.' " She stared at Bernadette's glasses and smiled. "No offense meant."

Bernadette said, "No offense taken."

"Did they also bring the blue blobs?" Chloë asked.

"Honey, they put them on at the TV station itself. That reporter never even mentioned that they would. I have half a mind to sue them for infringing on my First Amendment rights."

"What rights might those be?" Chloë asked.

"Why, freedom of speech, I think it is."

Bernadette laughed. "It's called freedom of expression, Wanda. You might as well learn the proper terms because I can tell, you're going to need to know them."

Chloë kept sniffing the air. The carport was filled with a familiar smell that she couldn't name. And then she recognized it. It was coconut. Coconut in the middle of the carport. "Is somebody baking cookies?" she asked.

Tyler said, "Heck, no."

"What is that smell?"

"Coconut oil. My momma and Aunt Wanda oil their body parts before they go to work. In their line of work, the sun is very hard on their skin."

Certain of Wanda's and Velma's body parts looked as glossy as Christmas-tree ornaments.

Wanda said, "Why don't you wear a T-back, Bernadette? You're in good shape for a woman of your years."

Bernadette smiled and shook her head. "No," she said, "there are parts of me that I don't care for the world to see."

"Now, that's just false modesty," Velma said.

"In my case, I would say, the modesty is well deserved." Bernadette smiled and promised to bring Tyler back in a couple of hours.

* * *

Chloë was furious with Velma and Wanda, and Tyler too. She was glad that she had a plan to show him up for the fool he was. Bernadette had been going to bed early since they got the highway route, and most nights they didn't even play cribbage. Chloë had been studying in the evenings, preparing for the conversation she was about to have.

Bernadette dropped them off by the curb instead of driving around to the back of the dollar-movie parking lot. As they walked back, Chloë asked Tyler what he was learning at the Bible school at the Church of the Endless Horizon.

"Stuff."

"Stuff?" Chloë asked. "Stuff is what you get in a Christmas stocking. What kind of stuff?"

"Bible stories."

"That can't be all that you study."

"Hymns. We learn a lot of hymns."

"There must be something else. Don't you have tests at your school?"

"Every school has tests."

"I'm talking about witch tests," she said. "Are you familiar with the witch tests?" she asked, emphasizing the word *familiar*.

"I am," he replied.

"Which ones are you *familiar* with?" she asked.

"You tell me which ones you know, and I'll tell you if they're right."

"Well, I know the reason witches don't go in the water. Even if they're teaching someone to swim, they don't go in over their heads. That's because witches don't sink. The water won't take them. You can bind them up. You can bind their arms, just the way that Bernadette's arm is all bound up in that cast, and they won't sink. That's because they've never been baptized by water, and the water rejects them."

Tyler said, "That's absolutely right."

Then Chloë said, "So you're *familiar* with that one?"

Tyler said, "I just told you I was."

Then Chloë asked, "Are you *familiar* with the way that Bernadette got Daisy?"

He said, "My aunt Wanda told me a little bit about it, but you go ahead and tell me your version."

Tyler hardly noticed that they were already back at the marked-off part of the parking lot before Chloë finished telling the story of Jake and Daisy. He sat down on the curb and made no effort to put on his skates. He was silent for a minute after Chloë had finished. Then he said, "I never thought Daisy was no normal dog. I reckon Daisy was Jake's familiar. A familiar is the animal form that a witch's spirit takes. Then when Jake died, his spirit left a spot for Bernadette's to pop right in. That's the way them things work."

"Are you just guessing?"

"Not at all. I tell you, Daisy is your auntie's familiar."

"Did your teacher also explain that a witch can only summon her familiars and have them do her bidding when she is at rest? Usually at night."

"Yes," Tyler nodded. "It happens at night."

Then, acting as if the thought had just occurred to her, Chloë said, "It's funny to hear you say that. Do you know Daisy sleeps at the foot of Bernadette's bed, and Bernadette won't let me or anyone—*anyone*—into her bedroom at night after she has closed the door to go to sleep."

"No wonder your aunt didn't want no tercel. She has that there dog. You have to admit it would be better to have a dog than a bird. People don't suspect a dog that much." Chloë smiled to herself. Tyler had fallen into every trap she had set. She was enjoying this. She just hoped it wouldn't be too easy.

* * *

Tyler skated circles around everyone at the dollar-movie parking lot. Someone had brought a ramp like the ones they put in doorways for the handicapped. By skating fast, a good skater could glide to the top of the ramp and sail off. Those who were *really* good landed on their feet. Tyler not only landed on his feet, he did a full turn after landing, skated into the center ring, and did a spin and a world-class Hamill camel. Chloë was awed. So was everyone.

* * *

When Bernadette picked them up, she said that she was stopping at the Dairy Queen to celebrate the good report she had gotten from the doctor. They ordered from the drive-through window. The girl handed Bernadette the cones, and she in turn offered them one at a time to Chloë and to Tyler. She passed them some extra napkins before pulling away from the window to a parking space. With her arm in a cast it was not easy for her to eat and drive at the same time.

Tyler unwrapped the napkin that had been around his cone and replaced it with a fresh one. Before he took the first bite, he bowed his head and asked the Lord to bless the food he was about to eat. Out loud.

"How come you didn't say a prayer before you ate pizza the other night?" Chloë asked.

"I just learned it at my Bible school."

"You mean they taught you a blessing for frozen custard?"

"No. We learned to thank God for the food we put in our mouths, and frozen custard is food."

Bernadette stopped licking her cone. She lifted her head, and Chloë caught her eyes in the rearview mirror. Bernadette lifted her eyebrows and smiled. Chloë smiled back.

Complaints about the T-backs arrived at the TV station within minutes of Richard Roebuck's first report. The first to complain was a Reverend Mr. Butler, who headlined the news the following evening. That tape runs as follows:

> THE REVEREND MR. BUTLER: We have put together a group to protest the wearing of T-backs. Our group will be called the Citizens Opposing All T-backs and will be known by its initials, *COAT*. COAT will gather names on a petition to pass a law forbidding the wearing of T-backs in this community. Mrs. Westbeth will lead the petition drive.
>
> RICHARD ROEBUCK (*to Mrs. Westbeth*): What are your plans for COAT?
>
> MRS. WESTBETH: Our goal is to see this ob-

scene form of dress made illegal. T-backs are not only immoral, they are un-American.

ROEBUCK: Do you intend to ban T-backs on the beaches?

MRS. WESTBETH: Certainly. The beaches are where this whole thing got started, by foreigners. They started it with the two-piece bathing suit, then they went to the bikini, then the T-back. And if you want to see how it will end up, you get yourself on a plane ride over to Europe and have a look. You'll find people walking those beaches in the full light of God's good sun without a strip on. Is that what you want for our town? Nakedness? I'm here to tell you, we have to get these T-backs off of these people if we're gonna see what's decent in this town."

The morning following the formation of COAT, Richard Roebuck showed up at Zack's. That was the first day that all the driver-servers, except Bernadette, Chloë, and Grady, wore T-backs to the commissary. Someone had given them the word, and that evening they were on the six o'clock news.

RICHARD ROEBUCK (*He is standing next to Wanda in front of a sign that says* ZACK'S MEALS-ON-WHEELS): We went out today for a response to Mrs. Westbeth. (*He holds the microphone up to*

Wanda's face.) Do you have anything to say about these accusations of indecency?

WANDA: I sure do. (*She smiles.*) I say to all you people out there, you dress-for-success your way, and I'll dress-for-success mine." (*She moistens her lips, smiles at the camera, turns on her high heels and walks away. The blue blob follows.*)

After watching this newscast, Chloë said, "I don't like Wanda very much. Or Velma either. And even if they look terrific wearing T-backs, I don't think they ought to wear them to work."

Bernadette laughed. "I don't like them very much either."

"Which? Wanda and Velma or T-backs?"

"I don't like T-backs, but if Wanda and Velma want to wear them, I think they should."

"What's going to happen next, Bernadette?"

"Next, we'll have the suit."

* * *

Tyler had asked if they could go Rollerblading at the dollar-movie parking lot again, and Bernadette had agreed to pick him up the following day. When she and Chloë got to Wanda's, he was waiting on the front stoop. He ran down to the car and told Bernadette that Wanda wanted to see her. "If she wants to see me," Bernadette said, "tell her to come on out to the car and take a look." Bernadette waited, not too patiently, as Tyler ran back to the house and back out again. "She's coming. My momma's coming too," Tyler shouted from halfway down the walk. "They said for you to wait."

"Did they bother to say *please*?" Bernadette asked.

"They might of," Tyler said. "But they sure do want for you to wait."

Bernadette stared out the windshield. "It's about the suit," she said. "He's here. I know he is."

Wanda bounced over to the car, leaned in the window on the driver's side and said, "Our lawyer wants to talk to you. He come on over to the house to discuss our case, and we told him you'd be by for Tyler, and he's been waiting to talk to you. Didn't think you'd mind."

"I do," Bernadette replied.

"Well, excu-u-u-u-se me," Wanda said. "You must realize that you are the lone holdout at our commissary."

Bernadette said, "I do realize that, Wanda."

Velma said, "I happen to know that it's a constitutional right to bare arms. It's in all the papers."

"Velma," Bernadette said, "bearing arms does not mean baring arms."

Velma looked puzzled. "You just said it. How can *baring arms* not mean *baring arms*?" She turned to Wanda and repeated. "Didn't she just say that . . ."

"Have your lawyer check it out," Bernadette suggested.

Wanda asked, "Well, Bernadette, are you coming or not?"

Bernadette said, "C'mon, Chloë. Might as well get it over with. Let's meet the suit."

The suit was sitting on the blue brocade sofa in Wanda's living room when they arrived. He got up as soon as Bernadette and Chloë entered the room.

"Hi, Bayard," Bernadette said. "I thought it would be you." She put her hand on Chloë's shoulder. "I'd like you to meet Miss Chloë Pollack. She's Nick's kid."

"Nick's kid," he repeated and extended his hand. "Bayard McKnight. Pleased to meet you, young lady." Chloë shook his hand.

Wanda said, "I didn't know you knew Bernadette."

"We had some dealings a while ago." He didn't offer any more explanation but asked, "How you been keeping, Bernadette?"

"Happy. Busy. Staying out of trouble," she replied.

"Was you in trouble before?" Tyler asked.

"Ms. Pollack was once involved in a protest. You know about protests, don't you, young man?"

Tyler shook his head.

Turning his attention to Bernadette, he said, "You know why I'm here, don't you?"

Bernadette replied, "I guessed."

"You know it is not my habit to check guesses, Bernadette, so I'll take a minute to review, if you don't mind." He wiped his forehead. His handkerchief was sodden. The air conditioner in the window was making *glug-glug* sounds like a kid drinking a glass of water too fast. Mr. McKnight had on his working clothes—a suit—and a half-moon of sweat darkened his jacket from shoulder to shoulder. "Mind if I sit down?" he asked. He was a tall man who did not look overweight as much as he looked out-of-condition.

Tyler quickly pushed a hardback chair over. The lawyer thanked him. "This is the story. The Reverend Mr. Butler's group, COAT, is asking the city to pass a law banning T-backs. The law would ban T-backs on the beaches and even in your own backyard unless you are under ten years old. I believe such a law would be a violation of our First Amendment rights to freedom of expression. Mrs. Westbeth, the reverend's first lieutenant in the army of COAT, has noticed that you do not wear a T-back, the only one at Zack's who does not . . ."

Chloë interrupted. "I don't. And neither does Grady. That's Grady Oates. He doesn't wear one either. That makes a total of three. Bernadette, Grady, and me."

Bayard grew testy. "Little lady," he said, "I don't believe COAT wants to sign up Grady Oates. He's an old man, and he's crippled, and no one cares if he wears a T-back. And much as you may not want to believe it, no one really cares if you do either." He looked at Bernadette. "But you—you, Bernadette Pollack—you are a different matter. You are at the top of the list of COAT's most wanted. COAT has concluded that you are the one driver-server who still has some morals."

Bernadette said, "Morals have nothing to do with it."

Bayard said, "I know."

Tyler said, "Does that mean that you'll be signing up with them COATs?"

Bernadette said, "No."

Tyler let out a sigh so loud it sounded like grown-up relief. No one but Chloë paid attention. She wondered why Tyler was relieved that Bernadette would not be joining COAT.

Bayard said, "The best thing for our side, Bernadette, would be for you to wear a T-back."

Velma added, "You wouldn't have to wear one every day."

"But at least once, so that the public can see solidarity," Wanda added. "I'll call the TV news when you do, and they'll see you're on our side."

Bernadette said, "I won't do that."

"Why?" Wanda asked.

"You need to tell us why," Velma added.

Bernadette said, "No, I don't."

Bayard asked Bernadette to at least make a statement that they could give to the press. She didn't answer immediately.

"Well?" Wanda said.

"Well?" Velma said.

"Well?" Bayard said.

"Can't you see she's thinking?" Chloë asked. "You guys are as bad as TV anchors. You finish each other's sentences, and you can't stand a minute of silence."

Bayard was extremely annoyed. Chloë's remark came too close to truth. "Miss Wanda and Miss Velma do not happen to be guys, little lady, and I do not happen to think I am at all like a TV anchor."

"Well, you are," Chloë replied.

"How so?"

"You act folksy without being family, without even knowing us very well, and you think we should be flattered just because you're paying attention."

Bayard McKnight's face went from Tender Pink to Blush to Borscht. And it was not from the heat. "I see your point, little lady," he said, "but I maintain that I am not like a TV anchor. They are never as grouchy as I am, are they?"

"Underneath the smiles they wear, I think they are extremely grouchy," Chloë said. "I watch smiles a lot."

Bayard knelt down—it wasn't easy—to level his eyes with hers. "That's a good thing to do," he said. "We lawyers find watching smiles very useful when we are picking a jury, but let me tell you something, little lady. The big difference between me and TV anchors is this: under their razor-cut, blow-dried hair, and behind their eyes, they think they are more important than the job they do, but I don't. I never have, and I never will. Will you be so kind as to remember that?"

"Will you remember not to call me *little lady*?"

"I will." He started to laugh, stopped, and said, "I certainly will."

Tyler said, "You can still call me *young man*. I don't mind."

Finally Bernadette spoke. She was not relaxed, but she was calm. "Wanda, Velma, listen up," she said. "I'm going to say this once and only once. Bayard, I expect you to understand." She paused and waited for their attention before continuing. "I think everyone has a perfect right to wear a T-back if she wants to. I also think I have a perfect right not to wear one if I don't want to. *And* I have an equally perfect right not to stick up for anyone who does. Now, if you want to know my thoughts about freedom of expression, I'll tell you those too. This is what I think about freedom of expression: As long as I am not running for public office or trying to influence anyone who is, I have the right to my opinions and an equal right not to express them."

Bayard said, "You haven't changed, have you, Bernadette?"

"Maybe I've just become more of what I once was."

"You already know how this is going to turn out, don't you?"

She nodded. "We both know." She reached out to shake his hand. "I wish you well."

He covered her hand with both of his. "I wish us both well, Bernadette."

Wanda said, "What is this? Some kind of code you two are talking?"

Bayard McKnight replied, "Not code, Miss Wanda. We're talking history."

14

They went directly to the dollar-movie parking lot, where Tyler soon gathered a crowd. Lesser skaters cleared space and stood around to watch as he stretched, bent, and shaped his body as if his muscles were spandex and his bones rubber. Tyler may not have been beautiful to see, but he was beautiful to watch. People coming for the late movie saw the crowd and came over to investigate, only to stay and watch. And Tyler didn't disappoint them. He put on quite a show. He skated fast, glided up the length of the ramp, sailed through the air, landed, and went into a dervish spin. The only thing missing from a star performance was a smile. If he didn't look grim, he looked smug.

Chloë began to wish he would fall.

And he did.

Just when it seemed that the crowd could get no bigger and Tyler could do no wrong, he fell. Coming off the ramp, he slipped, missed and went down on his back. He had done the same trick—to great applause—at least six times before, but this time he misstepped. He went down so hard he skidded forward for two or three feet before stopping, flat on his back, his T-shirt up around his neck, too hurt to move.

He lay there, motionless, staring up at the sky. There was pain in his eyes, but no tears. It grew as quiet as a pulse. Everyone stood back for a hushed minute before rushing forward. Bernadette was first. She waved everyone else back.

She knelt beside Tyler and quietly asked how he was. His voice was strained, but he didn't cry. He said, "I'll be all right."

Bernadette didn't try lifting him. She asked him to move his legs. He did. Then she asked him to move his arms. He did. She guessed that nothing was seriously bruised except his pride and his back. "He'll be all right," Bernadette called out to the others. They gradually fanned back out to the farther reaches of the parking lot, but no one did any serious skating after Tyler's fall.

Bernadette removed her skates and laid them aside. She stood over Tyler, letting her legs straddle him so that she could pull him up slowly and evenly, without jerking one side harder than the other. She inspected his back. There were a lot of bruises and road burns. Nothing deep. She said she would take him back to her house to clean him off and put a poultice on the scratches.

When they got to the car, she told Tyler to lie across the back seat on his stomach. "I have my own special formula for cuts and scratches," she said. "I'm the greatest spin doctor around."

* * *

When they got to the house, Bernadette tenderly helped Tyler out of the car. Chloë put Daisy on a leash and walked her twice around the block, glad to have something to do that took her away from Tyler. This was the third time she had wished for something to happen, and it had. She had wanted Bernadette to stop skating, and she did. She had wanted Grady Oates to answer the phone, and he did. She had wanted Tyler to fall, and he did. She had wanted Bernadette to stop but not fall; she had wanted Tyler to fall and be embarrassed, not hurt. The only one of the three wishes that had come out right had been Grady Oates. Two out of three times, she had not gotten it quite right. She decided that she would have to stop wishing for things that did not help others.

That settled, she worked on sorting out her feelings about Tyler. He was like a hangnail, more annoyance than pain. She was not having much success trying to ignore him. But she would try. She would sort out all her feelings, color-code them, line them up, put them in a closet, close the door, forget about them, and never go Rollerblading with him again.

Starting tonight, she would write long letters home. Since she was closing the door on that part of her life, she would write Angelica and Krystal and tell them about Tyler. She would tell them about his skill on Rollerblades. She would skip the overbite, the bad grammar, the fact that he didn't have even the beginnings of a beard (she had looked closely), and that he never thanked anyone except God for anything.

Chloë returned to the house and unleashed Daisy in time to see Tyler emerge from the bathroom wearing one of Bernadette's clean T-shirts and carrying his own soiled and stained shirt bundled in his hand. He announced that he was ready to go home.

Much to Chloë's surprise, she heard herself saying, "I'll ride along."

They sat together in the backseat. Bernadette tuned into the classical music station.

Tyler sat very still, but every now and then he tugged at the T-shirt to loosen it from sticking to his back. "That salve your aunt made sure is greasy."

Chloë replied, speaking in a low and mysterious voice. "She uses hyssops and eye of newt."

Tyler said, "Oh."

Before they got to Wanda's, most of the sting was gone, and Tyler leaned back and relaxed. He looked comfortable. Chloë said, "You'll probably be better by morning. When Bernadette decides to cure someone, she does."

"That being the case," Tyler asked, "why is her arm still in a cast?"

Chloë didn't even have to think before answering. "Her hand is better. You heard her say she got a good report from the doctor. She keeps the cast on to protect her sleight of hand."

"What's that?"

"Sleight of hand? You don't know about sleight of hand?" Tyler nodded. "I'm surprised your Bible-school teacher didn't teach you about sleight of hand." Tyler said they didn't. "Well, sleight of hand is what it takes to do magic with cards. I hope we get back home in time for me and Bernadette to play some. Bernadette is awfully good at it. She's used to winning all the time, but I'm acquiring the skill, and I win about one-third of the time now."

Tyler asked, "Did you say *eye of newt*?"

Chloë said, "Yes."

Tyler leaned back fully and appeared relaxed and free of pain. He said nothing more until they got to Wanda's and then, as he got out of the car, he said, "See you tomorrow."

"What?" Chloë asked. "You want to go skating tomorrow?"

"Sure. I like that dollar-movie parking lot, and my back's feeling better already."

And Chloë said, "Same time, then."

Mrs. Westbeth lived up to the promise she had made on TV. COAT began picketing the food-service vans on Talleyrand. Even though there were only a dozen people carrying signs the first day, they got a lot of coverage on the evening television news—both early and late broadcasts. Every station featured them, and the newspaper ran a picture of the picketers on the front page. By the end of the day, it seemed there were protesters everywhere—a lot more than there really were.

The news of the protest movement backfired.

An epidemic of T-backs broke out.

Sidewalk vendors—the men and women who sold ice cream and soft drinks from carts on downtown street corners—were next to wear them. The men and women who sold hot roasted peanuts in the ballpark parking lot followed. Before the week was out, every food vendor in town except Bernadette and Grady Oates wore a T-back to work.

No doubt about it, T-backs were good for sizzle, and no one was benefiting more than Zack. His drivers were making more money for him than they ever had in the entire history of his company. Everyone except Grady Oates and Bernadette. Grady's sales stayed the same, but Bernadette's were down.

Zack called Bernadette into his office again and asked her if she thought that he should change the brand of merchandise she was selling in the van since she didn't seem to be selling very much of what she had.

She said no.

He asked her if she would wear a T-back.

She said no.

He asked her if she wasn't willing to wear one because of the kid.

She said, "Do you mean because of *Nick's kid*, Zack?"

"Well," he said, "you have been known to change your loyalties because of a kid."

Bernadette said, "This is not because of a kid, Zack."

"You're putting me in a bad situation, Bernadette," Zack said. "There are a half dozen young ladies out there who are perfectly willing to put on a T-back and drive your route."

Bernadette said, "At least a half dozen."

"A young girl in a T-back could pull in twice the business you're doing." He waved the records in front of her.

Bernadette said, "At least twice."

Then he asked her if she would mind taking a job inside the commissary for the rest of the summer.

She said yes, she would mind.

"Very much?"

"*Very* much."

Zack said, "What am I gonna do with you, Bernadette?"

Bernadette replied, "You can keep me on, or you can let me go. Those seem like the two options you have."

Zack never really answered. He shrugged, sighed, and turned away.

* * *

Bernadette knew that Chloë had overheard her conversation with Zack, so that evening as they sat drinking coffee in the living room, she asked if Chloë would like to hear another story of how TV news was used to promote a cause. "Bayard McKnight was a part of it, and so was I—at first."

It was May 4, 1969. Bernadette was twenty-two years old and was one of thirty-six people blocking the entrance to the draft-registration office at the municipal building in Peco. What they were doing was illegal because it is against the law to block access to public buildings.

The thirty-six were trying to prevent people being registered for the draft. They figured that if no one went into the armed services, there would be no one to fight the war in Vietnam, so they chained themselves together and wouldn't let anyone into city hall, where the draft-registration office was. Everyone from Spinach Hill was there except Nick. He was only twelve, and he was in school.

One of the leaders had notified the news that the protesters were planning to start a bonfire to burn draft cards. That was the second illegal thing they were doing. They knew they would be arrested. Some had agreed to spend the night in jail, while others would have bail posted. Bayard McKnight was the lawyer who would defend the protesters. He had funds to post bail for those who did not want to spend the night in jail.

The rumor went out that someone had managed to get to the network news. Imagine! National coverage for the Peco protest. The leaders decided to wait for the network news team before starting the bonfire. They didn't want everything to be over before they showed up.

Bernadette had been designated as one for whom bail would be posted, so that she could get back to Spinach Hill. It got later and later and later. Every protest spawns an antiprotest, and while they waited for the network news team, the antiprotesters got organized. Picketers carrying signs saying HIPPIES GO HOME marched back and forth in front of city hall. The original protesters were excited when that happened because it meant the news of the Peco protest would be more dramatic. They waited, but still the network news did not show up. They never did, but no one knew that they would not. The rumor had been repeated so often that everyone believed it.

Bernadette kept checking her watch. Nick would be boarding his school bus; he would be walking the three blocks of unpaved road to Spinach Hill; he would be home. It got later and later and later. It was well past suppertime—getting dark—when she asked Bayard McKnight to be excused.

He reminded her that everyone had agreed to be arrested and booked.

Bernadette knew it was unfair to the others for her to leave, but it was more unfair to Nick for her to stay. She had not known that she would have to be gone after dark, after normal city hall hours. She was risking Nick's safety. Who knew what the antiprotesters were doing at Spinach Hill? Maybe they were surrounding the house and had Nick trapped in there. All kinds of crazy thoughts were going through her head, but the one thought that she had the most was that she did not want Nick to spend that night in the house alone.

Bayard McKnight had her excused. She left the protest. She was never booked. She promised Bayard that if he let her go, she would never again put herself in a position where he would have to rescue her from her choices.

Chloë said, "Nick never told me that part."

Bernadette answered, "He probably doesn't like to talk about it."

"Maybe he didn't think it was important."

Bernadette said, "Oh! I doubt that. He knows that that night changed my life."

16

Bernadette resented going back to Wanda's to pick up Tyler.

"You don't like Tyler, do you?" Chloë asked.

"Chloë, let me tell you three things I've learned." She counted them off on her fingers. "One: Don't tell your brother who to marry. Two: Don't tell your niece who to be friends with. And three: Don't sue Santa Claus for not bringing you a bicycle and expect him to show up in court."

When they got to Wanda's, they found Velma in the carport. Using the trunk of the car as a desktop, she was autographing Zack's price-list menu for two of the kids in the neighborhood. She signed it, "Love, Velma," and drew a smiley face inside the *o* of *love*.

Bernadette was listening to music in the front seat when Chloë asked Tyler how his back felt. He said that it didn't hurt at all. As a matter of fact, most of the scratches had already disappeared.

"Well," she said, "that's because Bernadette knows

what to put in her ointments. You can't buy the stuff a spin doctor makes. She has to grow most of it herself because no one is allowed to sell it commercially." Aside from hyssops, Chloë had no idea what Bernadette put in her poultice. She was simply reacting to Tyler again.

As much as he didn't want to, Tyler looked impressed, and that in turn encouraged Chloë. She continued, "Borage and hyssops create a condition of reverse osmosis. The flow of poisons can go one way or the other, depending on the order that Bernadette mixes them."

"I thought so," Tyler replied. "Your aunt is a witch, isn't she?"

At last Tyler believed.

Chloë did not answer yes or no. She stared into the middle distance with half-closed eyes and allowed her nostrils to flare. "Her powers have been known to infect those who live with her. Do you know why you fell yesterday?"

Tyler swallowed. "God was giving me a reminder. I fell from the path of righteousness. I allowed pride to come before my fall."

"That is not why you fell. Even people who don't go to Bible school at the Church of the Endless Horizon have heard *Pride cometh before a fall*, and that very well may be why some people fall, but that is not why *you* fell. You fell because I wished it."

"I've prayed for her, you know."

"For whom?" Chloë asked, emphasizing the *m* of *whom* so that Tyler would know that he was not dealing with an illiterate.

"I prayed for your aunt. Without mentioning any names, I got the whole school at the Church of the Endless

Horizon to help. It is our duty to raise our voices in prayer to save her poor bewitched soul." He leaned over to Chloë and whispered, "There is more."

"More what?"

"More proof that she's bewitched."

Chloë said, "I'm interested. I really am." She crossed her arms across her chest and leaned back. Here he was, acting as if he were the big authority on witches, and he wouldn't know anything if she hadn't told him. Tyler had to be the most irritating thing to come out of Georgia since fuzz off peaches.

Tyler glanced toward the front seat, leaned toward Chloë, and whispered. "There's the thing that Daisy done."

"What did Daisy do?" she asked.

"You know how she jumps up on Bernadette?"

"Of course I know how she jumps on Bernadette. That's what dogs do. They jump up on people they like, and they sometimes lick their faces."

"Well, I know that. But, get this: Daisy, she jumped up on Bernadette and scratched at her pap, and Bernadette didn't even know it."

"Well, of course she didn't," Chloë said, irritated that Tyler was about to tell her something she didn't know. "What's a pap?"

"A tit. The Reverend Mr. Butler, he calls them paps, and he says if you poke a witch in her paps and she don't feel it, it's because they are being used to suckle imps."

"Did the Reverend Mr. Butler happen to tell you what imps are?"

"He did. Imps is small demons. Witches suckle them." Tyler leaned back. "You can just relax, though, because I didn't tell him that it was your aunt what had the pap. I didn't give out any names."

"Well, that is very thoughtful of . . . ," Chloë said, and then stopped in midsentence. "Did you say the *Reverend Mr. Butler*?"

"I did. We must listen to him. He is head of the Church of the Endless Horizon and God's messenger here on earth."

Chloë remembered Tyler's sigh of relief when Bernadette said that she would not sign on with COAT. "Is that the same Reverend Mr. Butler who is head of COAT? The same one who is head of Citizens Opposing All T-backs?"

"The very same. What of it?"

Chloë said, "Well, if the Reverend Mr. Butler is leading the crusade against the T-backs and your mom and your aunt are leading the crusade for them, I think that's a pretty good *what of it*. As a matter of fact, I think that's a whopper of a *what of it*."

"Well, I did not tell him. The Reverend Mr. Butler don't know that Velma is my mom and that Wanda is my aunt. My last name is Blakely. And Mrs. Blakely was the name my momma used when she signed me up, even though she don't use it at other times because she ain't been married to my daddy for a long time. And no one at the Bible school knows which is my house because the bus picks me up on the corner two blocks away and drops me off at the same place, and it's none of their businesses neither. And the reverend, he don't need to know. And if he finds out, I'll know it was you who told."

"Does your Reverend Mr. Butler say it's all right to go skating with a witch?"

"I didn't tell the Reverend Mr. Butler exactly who was

taking me to the dollar-movie parking lot when I explained to him that I must undo all the prideful skating I done last night. It's my duty to skate tonight. God is testing me."

"And what did the Reverend Mr. Butler say to that?"

"He said *amen.*"

* * *

Something had gotten out of control. Chloë had never meant the information she was feeding Tyler to go beyond the two of them. She wasn't sure what or how it had happened, but she sensed that she had lost control of the situation. Like wishing Bernadette would stop and having her fall; like wishing Tyler would fall and having him hurt, something had gone wrong. She only hoped that this time no one would get hurt. But she had an uneasy feeling that someone would.

17

As the number of T-backs escalated, so did the efforts of COAT. They set up tables at supermarkets all over Peco and collected signatures on a petition asking the city to pass a law that would make T-backs illegal. They marched, toe-to-heel, in circles around the food-service vans, carrying picket signs and chanting, "Just say no to T-back business." Besides picketing the vans on Talleyrand, COAT also decided to picket the downtown vendors.

That was a mistake.

The downtown food wagons were small carts that were pushed by hand. They were scattered at various street corners, so it was easy to "circle the wagons" and keep people from getting through to buy food. The protesters were successful at stopping business, but they also stopped traffic.

The same laws that forbid blocking access to public buildings forbid picketing without a permit and deliberately stopping the flow of traffic on downtown streets, so Bayard had the protesters stopped. Mrs. Westbeth complained that it was the motorists who were gawking at the T-backs who were stopping the flow of traffic, but Bayard convinced the judge that there was no law on the books—and at that time there wasn't—that didn't allow T-backs, but there was a law that didn't allow pickets without a permit. It was the picketers who were causing a bottleneck by not allowing customers to get through. COAT had to call off its pickets.

COAT printed Day-Glo orange T-shirts that said, in big black letters, T-SHIRTS NOT T-BACKS, across the front and

across the back.

That too was a mistake.

Wanda and Velma themselves showed up wearing T-shirts.

White T-shirts.

Thin white T-shirts.

Wet, thin white T-shirts.

Wet, thin white T-shirts with nothing on underneath.

That night on the evening news, the blue blobs went north of the waist, and the next day the T-SHIRTS NOT T-BACKS campaign disappeared from the face of the earth. Wanda and Velma went back to their dress-for-success uniform of choice, and Mrs. Westbeth went back to command central to think of what to do next.

* * *

For the next week there was little change in the T-back war. Neither side strengthened its position. Then, on a slow news day, Mrs. Westbeth called a news conference. Every TV station in town covered it. She announced that she would enlist the help of the one virtuous woman and the one virtuous man who worked at Zack's Commissary. "We are calling Mr. Grady Oates and Ms. Bernadette Pollack to our side. In the name of decency, they must answer."

Wanda decided to make a call of her own. She called the TV stations and suggested that they show up at the commissary early the next morning. When Bernadette and Chloë arrived, they were surprised to see InfoNews and NewsCenter 5 already there—lights and cameras ready for action.

The cameramen kept following Bernadette, and the reporters kept making a nuisance of themselves, shoving microphones in her face.

Bernadette refused to talk to them.

Finally Chloë and Bernadette finished loading up. Feeling relieved that they would soon be on the road and out of camera range, Bernadette got behind the wheel of her van, ready to pull away from the loading dock. Suddenly she pulled back into her parking slot and cut the motor. "Something's not right," she said. Just then, Grady Oates drove in. Bernadette got out. Chloë followed. Grady Oates got out of his van wearing a tattered terry-cloth robe. Like a mismatched set of baseball bats, his bare legs, one natural, the other plastic and metal, stuck out below the frayed hem of his robe.

"What are you doing?" Bernadette screamed. "Do you have on what I think you have on under that miserable excuse for a robe?"

Grady nodded yes.

"Why, Grady, why?"

Grady shrugged.

"Who got to you? Who told you to wear a T-back?"

"Wanda. Said I had to do it for the good of the company. Said it was a question of showing solidarity."

Bernadette said, "Well, Grady, nobody is going to make you wear a T-back. You take my car and go home, change into your regular clothes, and come back. Chloë and I will load your van." With that, she put her hands on Grady's shoulders and turned him around and pointed him toward her car. She took her keys from her pocket and shoved them into his hand. "Now, go!" she said, pointing to her car.

"I don't want to make you late."

"Who's going to be late? Look over there," she said, pointing. "Chloë is already starting to load you up." She spun around, still holding Grady's shoulder and yelled, "Chloë! Chloë! Load Grady."

As curious as Chloë was about how Grady attached his artificial leg, she was grateful to Bernadette for sparing her having to see him in a T-back and also for sparing her from having to see that kind old man embarrassed. She ran inside, happy to start loading Grady's van.

When they finished, Bernadette signed the clipboard and added a note at the bottom. "Shame on you, Zack."

Looking over Bernadette's shoulder, Chloë said, "But Grady said that it was Wanda who told him he should wear a T-back."

Bernadette replied, "She said *for solidarity.*"

Chloë said, "That's also what she said when she asked you to wear a T-back. Remember?"

"Of course I remember. I remember because I don't think *solidarity* is part of Wanda's vocabulary."

* * *

They were on the access road to the interstate. Bernadette eased into the southbound lane. "Would you like to hear about solidarity?" she asked.

Bernadette had been very proud the day that the commune voted her and Nick in. The residents of Spinach Hill thought it would be *neat* to help raise a child, and she thought that there was nothing she wanted more than to share that responsibility. She had been taking care of Nick since she had graduated from high school. Commune living was in fashion all over the country at the time, and she thought that it was the answer to all the nuisance chores that come with just plain living.

Aside from the petty quarrels that came up among the members of the commune, the first few months seemed perfect, but it didn't take long for the glow to wear off.

First of all, Bernadette realized that there was a part of her that did not enjoy doing everything in full view of someone else. She needed more time alone than this kind of living could give her. Every day, for some part of that day, she needed a piece of time that was hers alone. To be alone.

And then, the night of the protest at city hall, she realized something even more important. She realized that by allowing Nicholas to become everyone's responsibility, he had become no one's. She could not allow *no one* to be there for him when he came home from school any more than she could allow *everyone* to help him with his homework and correct his grammar. By giving up some of her responsibility—both in the house and with Nick—she had lost some freedom of choice. For a while she had been thinking about leaving the commune, but it was the night of the protest that she knew she had to.

Bernadette and Nick left the commune, and within two months, Spinach Hill broke up. They all accused Bernadette of creating that first crack in their solidarity.

Chloë asked, "Do you ever see any of those guys?"

Bernadette answered. "I work for one."

"Zack?" she asked, astounded. "Zack was once a hippie?"

"Yep," Bernadette answered, smiling. "We ex-hippies come in many guises."

"Have you known him ever since?"

"Oh!" she said. "I hadn't kept in touch all the time. But about eight years ago, I got sick and needed some surgery. I couldn't go back to my old job at the auto-body shop. I had heard that Zack had started this business, so I asked him for a job. I started working for him right after I came back from the wedding, when Nick married your mother." She smiled. "That was the funniest wedding, wasn't it? I remember you insisted upon walking down the aisle with your mother . . . as if Nick were marrying you too. In a way, I guess he was."

Chloë laughed. "I was scared. I was supposed to go down alone, but I was scared. I guess it was a funny kind of wedding. I remember you being Nick's best man. Dressed in a tuxedo, with your hair cut shorter than Nick's. I had never before seen a woman as best man."

Bernadette said, "I was glad Nick asked me to be his best man. I certainly couldn't have been a flower girl or a bridesmaid."

Chloë said, "Your short hair looked very chic with the tuxedo. That's what all of Mother's friends said."

"I was lucky to have any hair at all," Bernadette said. "You know, I haven't cut it since."

Chloë said, "It sometimes looks very nice, though."

Bernadette laughed.

As they drove down the highway, Chloë said, "I think Nick liked living at Spinach Hill. He talks to me about it a lot. I also think he's proud of his tattoo."

"I'm not," Bernadette said. "I'm not at all proud of Nick's tattoo. He was only twelve when all of us were getting tattooed, and I let him. It seemed like a good idea at the time. I thought, How can I tell him no when we're all getting one? It was unfair pressure. That was something else I realized about communal living: Nick had to conform to standards that were theirs but not necessarily ours—his and mine. I thought that more people could give Nick more, but they couldn't. They certainly didn't."

"Did you get a tattoo?" Chloë asked.

"You betcha."

"Is that why you won't wear a T-back?"

Bernadette smiled. It was a sad smile. "Not really," she said.

* * *

The tape of that evening newscast shows the following:

> *Bernadette slams the door of her van and rushes out to Grady Oates. She is having a heated discussion with him, waving her arms. She shoves her keys at him, and the sound picks up.* "Now, go!" she yells. *The camera catches Chloë running back into the commissary after Bernadette yells at her. Grady walks toward the Firebird. The camera focuses on his mismatched legs, then on his face. He smiles and shakes his head no at the microphones. He tries to wave the microphones away.*

Since neither Bernadette nor Grady had spoken to the reporters, the reporters spoke for them.

> VOICE OF RICHARD ROEBUCK (*having been introduced as the star reporter of T-back news*): The lone holdout at Zack's Commissary, where the vogue for wearing T-backs started, is a Ms. Berna-

dette Pollack, a seven-year employee with the firm. Until this morning, Mr. Grady Oates, another long-time employee, had also refused to wear a T-back. However, this morning, when he chose to show solidarity with those vendors who did, he was attacked by Ms. Pollack. We have footage of Ms. Pollack's confrontation with Mr. Oates, and Mr. Oates's retreat. The child you see in the background is Ms. Pollack's niece.

The tape stops rolling, and the cameras are back in the studio. Richard Roebuck is sitting at the anchor desk to the right of Anchor I.

ANCHOR I (*leaning across the desk*): Have any of the workers at Zack's Commissary questioned having a minor working under these conditions?

RICHARD ROEBUCK (*facing the camera*): NewsCenter Five has learned that the child's aunt (he glances down at his notes) . . . a Ms. Pollack, is an independent operator. Zack, the owner of the commissary, has not put the child on the payroll. And as you have seen, the child's aunt refused to talk to us on camera.

ANCHOR I (*facing camera, looking serious*): Thank you for that report, Richard. That was reporter Richard Roebuck, who first broke the news of the T-back controversy, with an update on the developments from Talleyrand.

The first telephone call came before the next commercial message. The first one said that Bernadette was the only decent and moral person in her line of work. The second call, which followed immediately, said that she was indecent for allowing a child to work in a place where women exposed themselves.

When she hung up the phone the second time, Bernadette said, "It's a crazy world out there. For doing what I'm doing, I'm called moral by one person and immoral by another." The phone rang again. She took it off the hook and laid it down on the kitchen countertop without holding it up to her ear. "And neither one has a clue about what I was doing."

Chloë asked, "Do you think God has something like a big camcorder so that He can see what really happened? If God's camcorder could see into people's hearts, wouldn't God's voice-over be accurate?"

Bernadette said, "I would hope so."

The following morning—Saturday—Mrs. Westbeth, the chairperson of the Citizens Opposing All T-backs, came calling. She wore a flowered dress that looked like the wraparound cover of a large seed catalog; the background color of the dress matched the blue of her hair. From the flush of her cheeks to the dusting of talcum in the *V* of her bosom, she had the moist, warm look of a baby just awakened from a nap. With her came Deacon A and Deacon B. They were dressed alike in black suits, white shirts, and black ties. The deacons were tall; Mrs. Westbeth was squat. They marched up the driveway, three abreast, A on the right and B on the left. Deacon A carried a briefcase with the famous COAT petition. B had a camera.

After congratulating Bernadette for her performance on the evening news, Mrs. Westbeth said that she had tried calling, but the line was always busy, so she decided to come personally to have Bernadette sign the petition.

She confessed that she was very excited to have seen Bernadette at last answer her call and stick up for decency.

Without asking permission, she spread the petition out on the kitchen table. Deacon A took a pen from his inside jacket pocket, pointed it at Bernadette, and said, "We'd like you to pose with Mrs. Westbeth on one side, and your niece here on the other." He snapped his fingers high over his head and pointed to Deacon B. B took the cap off his camera lens; A took the cap off his pen. "Now," Mrs. Westbeth said to Bernadette, "if you'd like a minute to freshen up, we'd be happy to wait."

Chloë watched Bernadette's back stiffen. She waited to see which of her sides Bernadette would show Mrs. Westbeth: quiet stubborn or loud stubborn.

Bernadette chose quiet. She said, "There's no need for me to freshen up, Mrs. Westbeth."

"Fine, fine," Deacon A said. "Then we can get right to the photo op." He held his hand up again and snapped his fingers. Mrs. Westbeth pushed up on her blue hair, tugged down on her flowered dress, and sidled over to Bernadette. She rested one hand on the edge of the kitchen table and attempted to put the other one behind Bernadette in a comradely gesture.

Bernadette swung around and said, "Get your hands off me."

Mrs. Westbeth's chins quivered. "I was only . . ."

Bernadette said, "And get these papers off my kitchen table." She looked down at Mrs. Westbeth's hand resting on the table. Mrs. Westbeth drew her hand back as if it had been burned. "I'm not signing your petition."

Deacon A said, "But you must."

Mrs. Westbeth opened her mouth as if to say something, but she couldn't. Her chins fluttered hard enough to fan the air.

Deacon B tried to explain. "You must sign the petition to show that you are on our side."

Bernadette replied, "But I'm not on your side."

"But you are."

"No, I'm not."

Deacon B stood behind Chloë, laid his hands lightly on her shoulders, and said, "I know you are a loving and caring aunt who does not want her young and innocent niece exposed to such displays of vulgar nudity. I know that is why you do not wear a T-back."

"No, you don't know."

Deacon B said, "Then tell us why you will not."

"I don't have to wear one or tell you why I don't."

Mrs. Westbeth regained her composure. She said, "We must stop these T-backs, Ms. Pollack. Many community leaders have joined us. Many, Ms. Pollack. A great many. And many are really big people in Peco. Allow me to read you some of the names of those who have already signed our petition." As she reached for the petition, the flesh on her upper arms swung to and fro.

Bernadette said, "Don't bother."

"You are called upon to do this, Ms. Pollack. It is your God-given duty. T-backs are the work of the devil."

Bernadette remained calm. "The devil, you say?"

Mrs. Westbeth said, "First Thessalonians says we should abstain from the appearance of evil."

"T-backs don't appear evil to me."

"They are. They lead men off the path of righteousness."

"What about Lionel? Is he leading men off the path of righteousness?"

"Your point is a false one," Deacon B said, smiling cautiously. "I am a man, and I know the devil wears many disguises. It is our duty to recognize them and put up barricades along the newly paved roads to hell."

Bernadette said, "You sure can turn a phrase, Deacon, but I will not sign." Mrs. Westbeth started to say something, but Bernadette cut her short by walking in front of her on the way to the door. She opened the door and swept her good arm in front of her. "Y'all better get as good at turning around as you are at turning a phrase. I am asking you to leave and take your petition with you."

Daisy got up and moved toward Mrs. Westbeth, her laser stare focused, her neck and back straight. She growled so low in her throat that the sound seemed to come from a distant time. Mrs. Westbeth pulled her arms in close to her body and nodded to A and B. They gathered up their papers and left in a flowered blur.

Bernadette and Chloë collapsed on the sofa laughing.

"*The devil, you say*?" Chloë asked, perfectly mimicking Bernadette when she had made the remark to Mrs. Westbeth, and they both broke out laughing again.

19

Bernadette decided they should go to a wonderful restaurant for supper, a place on the beach south of the Ritz. They would get all dressed up and be elegant. Chloë decided to wear the party dress she had brought from Ridgewood and had never worn. Bernadette said she would wear her blouse with the ruffled cuffs.

Bernadette seemed to take a long time to get ready, and when she came out, she looked different. She had done a make-over! Her hair was not tied back, and it framed her face like a smoky cloud; the gray now seemed to make it lighter and brighter. And she wasn't wearing her glasses. Bernadette had contact lenses after all. Chloë was impressed.

"You do have good cheekbones and a good figure," she said. "Why don't you wear makeup and dress like that more often?"

Bernadette replied, "When I was your age—during that time I wanted everyone to call me Detta—when I was trying to be the image I saw in magazine. and friends' faces, I spent a lot of time looking into mirrors. But then I got over it. I decided to look in the mirror and look *for* an image, not *at* an image. It is important to find the face that is your very own. It's important to do it before makeup and make-overs. Twelve's a good time."

Chloë asked, "Are you saying you would never sign a hair contract?"

"I guess I am."

"I didn't either."

"I know," Bernadette said.

Chloë thought, Sometimes Bernadette is so smart I can't stand her.

* * *

They drove along the coast road on the way to the restaurant. The windows of the Firebird were down, and they enjoyed the strong salt flavor of the air. Traffic was unusually slow because of a detour ahead. When they got to the patrolman who was directing traffic, Bernadette leaned out the window and asked what was going on. The cop said there was a demonstration.

"Whose?" Chloë asked.

"Some group," he answered and waved them on.

Bernadette found a parking place about four blocks back of the beach road, and they walked down to the demonstration. Some people were carrying signs that said BAN T-BACKS or what had become the official COAT logo:

Others carried lighted torches.

Chloë said, "I knew it would be COAT."

Bernadette said, "I guess we didn't have to be rocket scientists to figure that out. There will be a bonfire."

"How do you know?"

"The torches. The beach. After the draft-card burnings, the city passed laws that won't allow bonfires anywhere else. Every time there is a rally at the beach, something or other goes up in smoke."

After a good crowd had gathered—Chloë and Bernadette weren't the only ones who had stopped—the Reverend Mr. Butler led everyone down to the beach. Bernadette said she would watch from the top of the tallest dune. "I'll meet you here when you're ready to leave," she said.

Chloë followed the crowd down to the beach. The reverend stopped halfway between the ocean's edge and the dunes. Driftwood was piled as high as a party tent. The protesters formed a circle around the pyre. Screaming against the sound of the surf, the Reverend Mr. Butler gave a short sermon about the evils of T-backs and how nakedness was next to Godlessness. Then, using a torch that someone handed him, he lit the heap of driftwood. The fire blazed. At a signal from the reverend, the protesters tossed bathing suits into the fire. There was a frenzy of bathing-suit tossing, and the flames leaped and fell, brightened and darkened as the citizens of COAT fed the fire.

At last there were no more bathing suits to throw, and the fire died down to where it gave as much heat as light. The people in the first circle crossed arms and held hands with those on either side of them and began to sing "We Shall Overcome."

Chloë stepped back. She started to leave when she saw Tyler. He was standing almost directly across the fire from her, his head turned, trying to grab the hand of the man to the left of him.

"Tyler!" she called. He did not look up. She called again. "Tyler! Tyler! Over here." He looked up; their eyes locked for just a second. There was something fierce in his look. Also something worried and lonely. Then he squinted across the fire, as if he couldn't see her clearly, and took the hand of the woman to his right and the man to his left. He raised his eyes and stared ahead, gazing at a wedge of dune that rose behind Chloë's head. He opened his mouth and sang.

Chloë did not move for a minute. Couldn't move. She wanted to make sure she had an accurate picture of the world's best young hypocrite. Hands to the left and right of her were reaching toward her, urging her to join them, but she didn't want to join hands. She didn't want to sing. She didn't belong to the front circle of COAT. As she turned to go, someone grabbed her shoulders. A woman lowered her face level with hers. It was Mrs. Westbeth. "Is that you, Chloë Pollack?" she asked. "What are you doing here?"

"Visiting," she answered.

"Did I hear you call to Tyler?"

"Me?" Chloë asked.

"Yes, you. I heard you call Tyler. How do you know him?"

"With all due respect, Mrs. Westbeth," Chloë said, "I think you ought to ask Tyler how he knows me." She shook her shoulders loose from the woman's grip and ran to Bernadette.

20

Chloë was badly shaken by her encounter with Mrs. Westbeth and by the sight of Tyler demonstrating against T-backs. She said nothing to Bernadette as they drove to the restaurant. Bernadette allowed the quiet to nestle between them.

When at last they were seated at the restaurant and had given the waiter their orders, Bernadette said, "Do you think you can stand another story, Chloë?"

"Sure," Chloë replied. "What is this one about?"

"About another bonfire."

"You already told me. Remember? You told me about burning the draft cards."

"No, this bonfire is much older and much more famous. It is so famous it has a name. It is called the Bonfire of the Vanities. Do you want to hear about it?"

About five hundred years ago, in the city of Florence, Italy, there lived a man named Lorenzo de'Medici. He was not a king. He was a businessman, but he was as rich and as powerful as any king. He lived in a beautiful palace, and although he had no official part in the government, he ran the city. No doubt about it, Florence was Lorenzo's city. Lorenzo loved poetry, music, and art. He believed—as many people in those days did—that looking at beautiful things or hearing beautiful poetry and music brought people closer to God.

Some of the philosophers in the Medici palace served as talent scouts. They would tell Lorenzo about talented young men they discovered, and Lorenzo would invite them to come live at his palace to perfect their art. One of the young men that Lorenzo sponsored was the talented son of a stonecutter. His name was Michelangelo Buonarroti.

About the same time that Michelangelo was invited to come live at the palace, one of Lorenzo's talent scouts heard about a monk named Savonarola, who was preaching some spellbinding sermons in the towns around Florence. Lorenzo couldn't invite him to come live in his palace because monks live in monasteries, but he did use his influence to have Savonarola transferred to the monastery in Florence.

Lorenzo believed that the human body was an expression of Godlike perfection. Painting or sculpting nudes was a way to show beauty or heroism or sublime spirit. For example, Michelangelo's giant statue of David uses a naked youth to express a heroic spirit, but where Lorenzo saw art, Savonarola saw wickedness. To him the human body was a source of shame. Actually, Savonarola saw shame and wickedness all around him. He thought Lorenzo was a heretic, a person whose beliefs were not officially acceptable to the church. And Savonarola also thought that the beautiful city of Florence was a terrible place, as wicked as Sodom and Gomorrah, because the people who lived there not only liked pleasure, they believed in it. Such beliefs, Savonarola thought, were heresy, and the people who held them were heretics. Of all the heretics, Lorenzo was the worst.

Savonarola claimed to be a prophet, a messenger sent by God, and he was a very convincing speaker. His sermons packed them in. Needless to say, he developed a very large following. They had to move him from the small monastery to the large cathedral in the heart of the city. Those on his side were definitely not on Lorenzo's. Some people claimed they saw angels at his side as Savonarola spoke.

Then, in 1492, Lorenzo de'Medici died, and Savonarola became the ruler of Florence. Like Lorenzo, he too had no official position, but he ruled the city from his monastery as certainly as Lorenzo had ruled it from the palace.

Once in control, Savonarola lost no time. He outlawed horse-racing, gambling, profanity, bawdy songs, and provocative female dress. He proclaimed dozens of fast days. Eating pastry was forbidden. And everyone—well, almost everyone—was enlisted as a spy for him. Children were encouraged to report on their parents, and servants were encouraged to report on their masters. But the best spies of all were a group of young men called the Youth Corps; they patrolled the streets of the city spying on everyone, looking for sin. They attacked gamblers, pastry sellers, and richly dressed women. If they saw a woman who they thought was improperly dressed, they sent her back home to change her clothes, and they had the authority to do so.

Savonarola believed that the people of Florence were particularly wicked just before Lent, during the time called carnival. In the year 1497, just before carnival, he sent his Youth Corps out to every household in the city to collect vanities. They gathered up cosmetics, playing cards, game tables, lace, jewelry, and books that did not make the monk's approved list. From the artists, the young men collected drawings of nudes. On Mardi Gras, the last night of carnival, a huge fire was lit in the city square and all these "vanities" were thrown on the fire and burned. And that was the first Bonfire of the Vanities.

That first Bonfire of the Vanities was so successful that Savonarola repeated it the following year. But the second one was not as good as the first. Sequels seldom are. By the time of the second bonfire, the butchers of the city were furious because there were so many fast days they were going bankrupt. The silk weavers were mad because no one was buying fancy fabrics. The artists couldn't paint nudes, and the artists' models were out of work too. The pastry makers had to close their shops. And the people—the users of these "vanities"—missed having beautiful things. Even if they couldn't own them, they missed seeing them. They missed having fun. Man, they said, is the only animal that plays as an adult. Would God have made us playful if he didn't want us to play?

The citizens of Florence organized. They arrested Savonarola, accused him of being a heretic. They said that he had misled the people of Florence. They tortured him, made him confess, and burned him alive in a great bonfire in the same city square where they had celebrated the two great Bonfires of the Vanities. They threw his ashes into the river.

Bernadette took a long drink of water, and Chloë absently twirled pasta around her fork. She had a lot to think about. "Who do you think tonight's bonfire will help the most?" Chloë asked. "COAT or the T-backs?"

"Both," Bernadette answered. "First it will help COAT, then it will help the T-backs. They cancel each other out. Bonfires have a way of getting publicity, and that's what they really want. I saw people with cameras there. COAT will make headlines, and that will help get more signatures on that petition, but when the T-backers see how many people are signing up, they'll try harder. It will fire up both sides just as our draft-card burning did, and just as Savonarola's Bonfire of the Vanities did five hundred years ago."

What Bernadette said made sense, but Chloë thought of Tyler's intense face and Mrs. Westbeth's angry one, and she suffered from a strange, sinking feeling that this bonfire was going to backfire.

The phone rang while Bernadette was in the shower getting ready for her follow-up appointment with the doctor. Chloë answered. It was Tyler.

"I've got to see you," he whispered into the phone. "It's important."

Chloë said, "We're practically not here. We are practically on our way to the doctor's office."

"Tell your auntie that you got to practice your skating."

"I told you not to call her my auntie."

Tyler said, "Tell her the same way you done the last time she went to the doctor's."

"I told you to call her Bernadette."

"You come on by and pick me up. Don't tell her I called." And he hung up. Chloë knew that she was about to learn the consequences of the Bonfire of the T-backs.

* * *

Tyler sat at the curb, staring at nothing. At last he spoke. "I got something to tell you." He pulled at the laces of his skates. He wouldn't look at her. "About the Reverend Mr. Butler, the head of our Bible school at the Church of the Endless Horizon."

"I know who he is."

"He found out."

"Let me guess. He found out who you are. He found out that the two star T-back wearers in the town of Peco, U.S.A., happen to be your mother and your aunt. Well, I didn't tell him."

"You as good as did. It was because you called to me the night of the bonfire that Mrs. Westbeth heard you. Old Westbeth knew who you were, and when she asked me how you knew me, it all come out that I had a connection with Zack's. It come out that I'm Velma's kid. Yesterday after school, he—the reverend—called me into his office, and after he established that I was child to one and nephew to the other of the T-backers, he said as how the Lord done to Adam and Eve, casting them out of the Garden of Eden in their nakedness, he was gonna have to cast out my momma and me right along with her. He called my momma a sinner, and he said I was a child of sin. I didn't like that. So I told him that Adam and Eve wore fig leafs and what my momma was wearing was covering more than any fig leaf ever did, and he might could think of my momma's mode of dress as *biblical.*"

The Reverend Mr. Butler told Tyler that he was like the devil quoting scripture to make a point. That evening he paid a visit to Wanda's house and told both Velma and Wanda that they would have to stop wearing T-backs, or he would expel Tyler from Bible school. He stated that he could not allow the child of a woman with no virtue to come to his school.

Wanda told the reverend that only people with distorted minds believed that exposing the body was disgraceful. She said that it was her personal belief that since her body was given to her by God, it was a form of God-given beauty, and her lawyer had told her that wearing a T-back was a form of artistic expression.

It was the reverend's personal belief that bringing God and lawyers together in the same sentence was another form of the devil quoting scripture to save his soul. The Reverend Mr. Butler became quite heated and raised his voice and told Wanda that she was a disgrace to her work and her family. He threatened to get COAT to close down Zack's place since that was where this epidemic of evil had started, and that was where it ought to end. He said that there was only one woman of virtue in all of Zack's place and that one woman was Bernadette Pollack, and he was sorry that she would have to lose her job along with everyone else when he closed them down.

"And that's when I told him," Tyler said.

"Told him what, Tyler?"

"About Bernadette."

"Told him what about Bernadette, Tyler?"

"Told him about how Bernadette is a witch, and that if he was on the lookout for evil, he didn't have to look no further than Bernadette."

Chloë was speechless. When she recovered her wits, she said, "Evil? How can you call Bernadette evil?"

"Because she's a witch. You know that your ownself. And witches consort with the devil. And the devil is evil, spelled with a *d*."

"And what did the Reverend Mr. Butler say?"

"He tried to make out like he weren't surprised. He said that he knew there would be some reason why Ms.

Pollack had ordered Mrs. Westbeth and the deacons out of her kitchen. The reverend had been pretty heated up about that. Mrs. Westbeth, she had already reported to him about that spooky dog of your auntie's, and she told him how she seen you stare at the bonfire like you was under some kinda spell. The reverend, he didn't take too much convincing after that."

Tyler finished lacing his second skate. He stood up. "My momma don't want me to get throwed out of the Bible school. Aunt Wanda says she don't have any idea what she's gonna do with me all day if I get throwed out. And the Reverend Mr. Butler won't throw me out as long as he needs my help. And I'm making sure he's gonna need it to investigate your auntie."

"Don't call her my auntie. No one calls her that. She's Bernadette, plain and simple."

"She may be plain, but she ain't so simple." With that, Tyler skated away.

Chloë thought, Surely no one believed that Bernadette had made a pact with the devil. No one except the Reverend Mr. Butler. The Reverend Mr. Butler and Mrs. Westbeth. The Reverend Mr. Butler, Mrs. Westbeth, Deacons A and B, and all of the Bible school at the Church of the Endless Horizon and all of COAT. They all believed that Bernadette was a witch. They all found evil in as many places as Savonarola did. In T-backs, in nakedness, in witches.

She knew now that she had totally lost control of the situation. She had first sensed she was losing it when Tyler had asked everyone at Bible school to pray for Bernadette. She should have stopped her little game right then and there, but she hadn't. Now, thanks to her, Tyler had all the evidence he needed to convince the reverend and his congregation that Bernadette was a witch. Tyler would not only save his place in the Bible school but would also save his mother's job. Instead of being a fool, he would become a hero.

Once again, what she had wished for had come about, but again things had developed a strange twist. She had managed to line everyone up against Bernadette: the T-backs, the suit, and COAT. And all Bernadette had ever wanted in this whole T-back war was to stay out of it.

* * *

Chloë didn't get a chance to say anything more to Tyler. He was skating circles around her and everyone else. When Bernadette picked them up, Tyler said, "I don't want no Dairy Queen tonight." That was all he said. He left the car without a good-bye or a thank you.

22

On the day that Bernadette went to the doctor's to get the cast taken off her wrist, she dropped Chloë at the dollar-movie parking lot. Tyler was already there. "I been here just about every evening this past week," he bragged. "I told Aunt Wanda about this place, and she's been dropping me off on her way to Zack's in the evening."

"How's your investigation coming?" Chloë asked.

"You'll find out soon enough."

From that moment on, Chloë was uneasy.

* * *

Bernadette was so pleased to be free of her cast, she said that they would celebrate with a candlelight feast on Sunday evening.

Because it was not yet dark when she lit the candles, she pulled down the shades to make the candlelight more dramatic. Her arm looked limp, thin, and discolored from having been in the cast, but she told Chloë that she had conquered things worse than a sick arm. Helped by Bernadette's good spirits and the romantic candlelight, Chloë entered into a feeling of celebration for the first time since Tyler had told her about the reverend's investigation. The candles were still burning and they were about to clear the table when Daisy assumed her guard dog stance.

Chloë knew that company was coming, and she felt that the end was coming too.

She went to the window, pulled the shade aside, and watched the Reverend Mr. Butler emerge from the driver's side of a long gray Cadillac. Zack came from the passenger's side; Tyler, Velma, and Wanda, from the back. They all proceeded slowly up the path to Bernadette's front door. They were all dressed up; Zack, Tyler, and the reverend wore suits. Velma and Wanda wore long silk dresses, buttoned up to the neck, tied at the waist.

The reverend carried his Bible; Wanda carried a camcorder; Velma, a camera. Tyler carried the T-shirt that Bernadette had loaned him the night he fell at the parking lot. It had been washed and ironed. Tyler handed it to Bernadette as soon as he was inside the door. Zack, the last one to enter the house, carried nothing, but he would not look at Chloë or Bernadette. He kept his head down and mumbled hello.

The candles still burned in the kitchen. Bernadette snuffed them out one at a time. The kitchen looked dark and smoky, and the odor of wick and wax wafted into the living room, where the guests now stood. The smell penetrated the room, causing the Reverend Mr. Butler to lift his nostrils. He sniffed the air and exchanged a knowing look with Tyler. To dispel the gloom more than the dark, Chloë turned on every lamp in the room.

All of them sat down except the reverend. He remained

standing, Bible in hand, and began to speak in a voice that was half political candidate and half talk show host. "Mrs. Pollack . . . ," he began.

"Ms. Pollack," she corrected.

"Yes, Ms. Pollack," he continued. "Some serious charges have been brought against you."

"By whom?" she asked.

Chloë knew what was coming.

The Reverend Mr. Butler did not answer her question. Instead he drew a deep breath and said, "Ms. Bernadette Pollack, you stand accused of being a witch."

Bernadette laughed. "You're not serious."

"I assure you, Ms. Pollack, I am very serious."

Bernadette smiled. "Who says I am a witch?" she asked.

The reverend answered. "A little child."

Bernadette shot Chloë a glance, and Chloë returned a startled look. She would have to confess. She was ready. She would tell them how she had deposited every piece of information that Tyler had in his memory bank. But the reverend said, "Young Tyler here has witnessed. He has brought us evidence."

"Evidence? Evidence?" Bernadette said. "What evidence?"

At that, Tyler leaped up from his chair and stood in the center of Bernadette's living room and recited all the evidence that proved that Bernadette was a witch. He had it all memorized. More than that, he had it all rehearsed.

- Bernadette wouldn't attempt to swim because she had made a pact with devil. The water would reject her because she had not been baptized.

- She had bewitched a dog to act as her familiar, and she communicated with it every night in her bedroom.
- She made magic potions from herbs and roots and wild mushrooms, and some of them could cure, but others could make you sick.
- She did magic with cards.
- She had a pap that suckled imps and could not feel when scratched by her familiar.
- She had a tattoo of the anti-Christ on her body.

After each item, Velma and Wanda nodded and said *amen* and the Reverend smiled.

Chloë's head felt like the contents of a table at a garage sale where all the odds and ends are laid out. There was something there in the assortment of Tyler's junk that she wanted to pick up and examine. What was it? Something didn't belong on that table. She didn't have time to concentrate because Tyler was still talking. She heard her name.

- . . . trained her apprentice, Chloë, to do magic with cards and to put curses on people, causing them to fall from grace.

Bernadette stood up. Chloë thought, Now Bernadette knows. She's figured out that I bragged to Tyler about having learned to put a spell on someone.

Bernadette faced her accusers. From one to another she

looked, and waited for a reaction from each before allowing her gaze to move on. Wanda stared vacantly into space; Velma tried to smile; Zack looked at his lap and flicked lint from his trousers. The Reverend Mr. Butler, who had remained standing, lifted his chin and raised his eyes in an effort to be on a par with Bernadette. Tyler took a tiny bow.

At last Bernadette spoke. "Reverend, I congratulate you on your Youth Corps. Savonarola could not have trained him better."

The reverend said, "Thank you. Now, I must ask you to offer proof that you are not a witch." He held up a piece of paper. On it was a drawing of Nick's tattoo. Chloë wondered, Why did the reverend want to know about Nick's tattoo? He waved the paper under Bernadette's nose. "Ms. Pollock, you must explain to those of us gathered here why you have an upside down broken cross, a sign of the devil, tattooed on your body."

That was it. That was the piece of information that Chloë needed to examine. She had never mentioned the tattoo to Tyler. Why would she? It was not the sign of the devil. It was the peace symbol. Chloë took the drawing from the reverend and examined it. It was the same as Nick's tattoo. Exactly the same. If a person wanted to, he could make it out to be an upside down broken cross as easily as he could make it out to be an anchor or a bow and arrow. But it wasn't. It was, pure and simple, the sign of peace. Nick was proud of his. He had said that everyone at Spinach Hill was proud.

Without a please or a thank you, the Reverend Mr. Butler snatched the paper back from Chloë, waved it in the air, and hissed, "Confess! It is because you bear paps that suckle imps and the mark of the devil that you will not wear a T-back. Confess!" The Reverend Mr. Butler was getting very heated. "Prove to us that you are not an emissary of Satan. Prove to us that you do not bear the mark of the devil upon your person."

And then realization hit Chloë. Zack! Zack was the only person there who would know that Bernadette had a tattoo. He had lived at Spinach Hill when they all got them. Zack knew what it was.

Chloë heard a voice say, "Excuse me." She heard it again. "Excuse me," it said. She saw all eyes in the room turn to her before she recognized the voice as her own. She looked at Zack, and Zack began to fidget. She let him. She let all eyes shift to him before she said, "Zack, I think that if you want Bernadette to show the reverend her tattoo, you ought to show him yours."

Zack reamed his collar with his fingers, stretching his neck so that his Adam's apple rested above his collar like a flesh-colored echo of the knot of his tie, but he didn't answer. Wanda looked as uncomfortable as Zack. She had seen Zack's tattoo. She knew he had one exactly like the one he had drawn on the paper the reverend was holding.

The Reverend Mr. Butler paid no attention to Wanda, Zack, or Chloë. He was not interested in finding out about the tattoo. He was only interested in confessions. He raised his right arm and extended his hand, holding the Bible. "Swear to us," he said, "swear to us on this Holy Bible that you are not an unholy woman bearing the mark of the devil."

"What makes you think that Bernadette has to swear to anything?" Chloë asked. The question came from a mysterious place deep within her, a place that rose in her throat the way that Zack's Adam's apple rose in his.

"My dear young lady," the reverend said, "please be still. This is a matter for the adults."

"Then why did you listen to Tyler?" she asked. Wanda started to answer, but Chloë wouldn't let her. "I asked *him*," she said, pointing to the reverend. She felt like a conduit, like a pipeline for the things that some stronger, older Chloë wanted to say.

The Reverend Mr. Butler said, "Tyler has witnessed for God, little lady. We must pay attention. Wherever evil lurks, we must seek it out and eradicate it from the face of the earth. Satan is the daddy of all evil, and in the name of God, your aunt must answer." The reverend faced Bernadette. "Ms. Pollack," he said, "I am asking you once again to prove to me that you do not bear the sign of the devil on your body."

Bernadette smiled, and then suddenly the smile dropped from her face like pudding from a spoon. "Reverend," she said, "I owe you nothing. Whether or not I have this sign tattooed on my body is my business. Not yours. Not Tyler's." She pointed to Velma. "Take your camera and your camcorder back with this message: I don't owe anyone here free footage for the TV news. I will not make a spectacle of myself. I do not owe that to anyone."

Tyler would not give up. "What about the pap? I seen that dog scratch at her and her not even feel it. I seen it."

Bernadette looked down at Tyler and said, "You poor nasty little boy. You poor toy of these people's greed." She walked to the door and opened it. She made a sweeping motion with her pale, weak arm. "I must ask all of you to leave my house. Now." She held open the door and stood majestically to the side as they filed out, one by one.

When the last of them was through the door, Bernadette leaned against it, exhausted. Behind her glasses her eyes burned hot enough to light tinder.

"Doesn't Zack have a tattoo?" Chloë asked.

"Of course he does. He got one when everyone who lived at Spinach Hill did."

"Why didn't you tell on him?"

"For reasons historical and personal." She leaned against the wall and crossed her arms at her waist. "Let me ask you this, Chloë. Would having Zack show the reverend his tattoo prove that I am not a witch?"

Chloë said, "But it would show that Zack is one too."

Bernadette threw up her hands. "There you go."

Chloë lay awake thinking. Everything that could go wrong had gone wrong. But she was safe. No one would ever find out the part she had played. Tyler wanted the Reverend Mr. Butler to think that he had done it all himself. He would never tell anyone that she had planted all but one of those magic seeds in his mind. She tried congratulating herself on getting away with it, but she couldn't. She found it harder and harder to convince herself that she should be allowed to get away with it.

She would confess.

Once she made the decision to confess, it became a need.

She would tell Bernadette everything. She would tell her what she had done and what she had not done. She had never—never once—mentioned the devil. Those accusations had come from the reverend's own warped mind.

Bernadette would find the whole thing very funny.

She, Chloë, would apologize.

They would both have a good laugh, and then she would get a good night's sleep.

After thinking and pacing, pacing and rethinking, she walked to Bernadette's room and timidly knocked on the door. Not too loudly, half hoping that she would be asleep and would not hear. But Bernadette answered immediately, and Chloë asked if she could come in. "Is this an emergency?" Bernadette asked.

"I'm not dying of gunshot wounds, if that's what you mean."

"I'll meet you in the living room," Bernadette said.

Bernadette appeared in the living room wearing a seersucker robe. Both looked tired and worn. "You want to confess, don't you?" Chloë sat on the edge of her chair, her mouth open. How did Bernadette know? "Is that it?" Bernadette demanded.

Chloë said, "Well, yes . . ."

"Do you have anything to say that I don't already know?"

Chloë shrugged. "I don't know what you know."

Bernadette said, "This is your confession, not mine. You speak."

Chloë sat on the edge of her chair and related how, in order to entertain herself, she had convinced Tyler that Bernadette was a witch. She enjoyed confessing not only because she was getting everything off her chest but also because she was rather proud of how cleverly she had turned the facts of Bernadette's life into flights of fancy.

When she was done, Bernadette asked, "Is that it?"

Chloë said, "Well, yes." Bernadette did not move. "What are you going to do?" she asked.

"Go back to bed."

"Are you mad at me?" Chloë asked.

"Yes, I am," Bernadette replied.

Chloë was dumbfounded. She had expected Bernadette to put an arm across her shoulder—not that she ever had before—and tell her that everything was all right. She was not getting the understanding she had expected. She struck out. "Well, Bernadette," she said, "there is an awful lot about you that is spooky by anybody's standards. Like how could you explain Daisy's behavior when Jake died?" As if on cue, Daisy growled. "And how can you explain the pap?"

"You stupid child," Bernadette said.

"Don't call me stupid."

Bernadette narrowed her eyes. "You are stupid. Your name for what you don't understand is spooky. My name for it is stupid. Stupid." She almost spit out the final word. She crossed her arms across her lap as if stricken with stomach cramps. She leaned forward and pushed herself up from the sofa. Bernadette looked as if she were on the verge of tears, and that frightened Chloë.

As Bernadette got up from the sofa, her robe gaped open, and Chloë saw that, under her robe, one side of her chest was totally flat.

Bernadette did not look at Chloë again. "Come along, Daisy," she said, and without a backward glance the two of them left the room.

Chloë at last put it all together. Bernadette had been "very sick" before Nick and her mother had gotten married, and at the wedding Bernadette's hair had been short enough to comb with a suede brush. It was just growing back after she had lost it all from chemo. That solved the mystery of the pap. On the night that Tyler fell, Daisy could scratch at Bernadette's left "pap," and Bernadette would not feel it because there was no pap. There was no flesh and blood where there had once been cancer. There was padding.

So that was why Bernadette wouldn't wear a T-back or a bathing suit. Bernadette in a T-back would be like Grady Oates in one: a combination of curiosity and embarrassment. Chloë threw her head back against the sofa and wailed at the ceiling. "Oh, oh, oh, I am stupid. A stupid child."

Chloë sat very still and thought. She couldn't let things rest like this. She knew now what they could do. They could get Bernadette's medical records—X rays and reports of her chemo—and show that she had had a mastectomy. After all, a lot of famous women—movie stars, presidents' wives—had had one, and there was nothing to be ashamed of. In that way, Bernadette could keep her privacy and still prove that she had no pap.

She got up from the sofa, marched straight to Bernadette's room, and pounded on the door. "Get up, Bernadette," she said.

Bernadette swung open the door. She was still in her robe. She had also stayed up thinking. "Is this an emergency?" she asked.

"Yes, it is. We have to talk."

"Come in," Bernadette said, opening the door wider and inviting Chloë in. There was only one chair in the room. Chloë took it. Bernadette sat on the edge of her bed.

"I figured out about the pap," she said. "I'm sorry I was so stupid."

Bernadette replied, "I do accept your apology, but let

me tell you three things I don't accept." She counted them off, raising her fingers one at a time. "Sympathy, lectures about how I shouldn't be embarrassed, and late-night conversations with twelve-year-olds."

Chloë settled deeper into the chair. "I'm not going," she said. "You invited me in, remember, and I think you want to listen to what I have to say." Daisy chose that minute to get up and rub against Chloë's legs and rest her head in her lap. Chloë automatically reached down and patted her. She whispered, "Good girl. Good girl. Bernadette and I have to talk, don't we?"

Bernadette swung her feet up on the bed, inched her way back to the headboard, and crossed her arms over her chest. "I'm listening," she said, not too kindly.

Chloë said, "The way I figure it is this: Your pap explains everything. Why you won't wear a bathing suit, why you won't wear a T-back, and why you won't show anyone your tattoo."

Bernadette said, "I don't have a tattoo."

For the second time that night, Chloë was dumbfounded. "What?"

Bernadette repeated, "I don't have a tattoo. My tattoo was on my upper arm. When I had my mastectomy, they had to remove some lymph nodes under my arm, and when they sewed up the fold of flesh, my tattoo got lost. There's only a small arc of the circle left."

"That changes everything."

"It changes nothing."

"That's where you're wrong, Bernadette. You can show them that you don't have a tattoo, and the doctor's reports will show that you don't have a pap. Zack will have to back off all this witch talk. . . ."

"That's where you're wrong, you stupid child. Zack knows about the so-called pap just as he knows where my tattoo was. And he knows about the surgery too. You just don't seem to get it, Chloë. My not having a tattoo no more proves that I am not a witch than Zack's having one proves that he is." Then Bernadette said, "Daisy will show you to the door. We need to get some sleep around here."

Chloë got up from her chair and walked the few steps to the side of the bed. She sat down on the edge of the bed and looked at Bernadette until Bernadette looked back at her. "Please, may I hug you?" she asked.

The time to touch had come.

Bernadette did not hesitate. Her arms reached out to Chloë, and their arms went around each other.

They hugged, their arms tightening and tightening as the unexpected became comfortable and then comforting. Daisy nuzzled between them, and still they did not let go of each other. Chloë knew that more than anything in the world, she loved this feeling. At that moment, she loved being three-in-one more than she had ever loved anything.

They held each other close for a long time. A long, long time.

Chloë got up early—she had hardly been able to sleep anyway—scurried around, set the table, brought in the morning paper, started the coffee, was more helpful than a whole ship's crew. She had gotten used to being helpful, but the unexpected was something else. How could a person give the unexpected a chance when it kept happening? How could anyone be expected to know that Bernadette no longer had a tattoo?

Bernadette was a little awkward with Chloë when she first got up. Chloë quickly went to Bernadette, hugged her around the waist, and planted a kiss on her cheek. Bernadette returned her hug, then pulled back looking embarrassed and said, "No time for mushy stuff this morning. There's work to do."

When they got to the commissary, they got the silent treatment. No one would talk to either of them. The air inside was charged enough to light up Chicago. They were not just made to feel unwelcome, they were shunned.

Bernadette said, "Chloë, darling, if they choose to divide the world between them and us, I'll take us."

Bernadette had never called her *darling* before. Never. And Chloë knew that she had helped Bernadette with more than chopped onions.

They went directly home after work.

Bernadette wanted to take Daisy for a walk. Chloë understood that she needed to be alone, and Chloë too welcomed a chance to think. She took a minute to stand by the back window and watch. Bernadette released Daisy from her leash and let her run free in the field behind the house. Daisy scampered back and forth as Bernadette meandered slowly farther and farther into the woods.

Chloë came away from the window. She had to think of a way to help Bernadette get out of the mess she, Chloë, had created. She was surprised to hear a car pull up into the driveway. She forgot how accustomed she had become to having Daisy warn them if someone was coming.

It was Bayard McKnight. He asked to see Bernadette, and when Chloë told him that she was not there, he asked if he could come in and wait.

Chloë was not only glad to have company but glad that it was Bayard. She wanted to know something about the law. "How do you prove that you are not a witch?" she asked.

He laughed. "The same way I prove that I don't beat my wife."

"But you're not married."

He replied, "And that's about the only way a person can prove he doesn't beat his wife."

"You're not very helpful." She wasn't being sarcastic. She was worried.

"It's easier to prove what you are than what you are not. That's why our courts always assume that a person is innocent until proven guilty. I really don't know how you prove that you are *not* a Communist or that you are not a wife beater . . . or not . . ."

"A heretic," she added.

"What do you know about heretics?" he asked.

"I know about the Bonfire of the Vanities."

Bayard asked if she knew about Galileo.

"Is this a test?"

Chloë said she only knew that Galileo had had a telescope and proved that the earth revolved around the sun.

"Did you also know that he was accused of being a heretic? Would you like a few of thc details? We suits earn our living from details."

Galileo was born in 1564, the year that Shakespeare was also born and the year that Michelangelo died. Even though people had gotten over their fear of vanities and nudity, they still worried about people who held controversial opinions.

Galileo turned his telescope toward the heavens and discovered that the earth revolved around the sun, not vice versa. He published his findings in a book. The pope called his findings heresy. Was it not written in the Bible: *The Sun also ariseth, and the Sun goeth down*? Did Galileo mean to say that the Bible was wrong?

In 1633 the punishment for heresy was death. Galileo was threatened with torture and brought to trial. He confessed. Kneeling before his judges, Galileo confessed to being a heretic. He was not hanged, but he was put under house arrest for the rest of his life.

Legend has it that when Galileo rose from his knees, after being sentenced, he muttered, "Nevertheless, it moves."

Chloë was puzzled. "How can they call him a heretic when everyone knows that the sun stays still and the earth revolves?"

"They can call him a heretic because at the time his opinion differed from that of the church. The church believed what the Bible said, and Galileo believed what he saw through his telescope."

"Couldn't the pope's men look through the telescope and see for themselves?"

"I suppose they could have if they had wanted to. But that's not the point, Chloë. The point is that Galileo could not prove that he was not a heretic because each age makes up its own definition of heresy. Joan of Arc refused to wear women's clothes, and that was heresy. Imagine that! Or think of this: People who claimed they saw angels at his side as Savonarola spoke were calling him a heretic a few years later. Three hundred years ago in this country, men and women in Salem, Massachusetts, were arrested for being witches. They were put on trial. None of them could prove that they were not witches. None. Like Galileo, those who confessed were not executed."

Chloë was fighting back tears of frustration. "Are you

saying that Bernadette should save herself by confessing to being a witch?"

"Not at all. I am saying that people always accuse someone with different views of being a heretic or a witch—or whatever—when they are worried about losing."

"Losing what?" Chloë asked.

"What it always is. What it always has been. Control or profit. Control, in the case of COAT. Profit, in the case of Zack. If Zack shows that his one holdout is a witch and that is why she won't wear a T-back, the reverend has to back down. Zack fires Bernadette to show that he doesn't mess with witches. Wanda and Velma look virtuous by comparison, Tyler stays in school, Zack makes more money. With Zack it's all business."

Chloë said, "I can't believe that Zack would do this to Bernadette just to make money."

"Not just fortune. Fame *and* fortune," Bayard said. "Zack is ambitious. He loves making news as much as he loves making money."

Then Chloë asked, "If there's no way Bernadette can prove she's not a witch, does she have to embarrass herself trying? Isn't there some law against harassing heretics?"

That question brought Bayard McKnight to his feet. "I think we need to find out."

Chloë asked, "Are you going to help Bernadette?"

"I am. I most certainly am."

"Aren't you going to be Wanda's lawyer anymore?" she asked.

"Zack, not Wanda, hired me."

"Zack?" she asked.

"Oh, yes. Zack."

"I can't believe that Zack hired you. I thought you took this case for free to defend Wanda's civil liberties, the way you defended the protestors of Spinach Hill."

"No. Zack hired me."

Chloë interrupted. "Bernadette must have known that. She told me that *solidarity* was Zack's word, not Wanda's."

"Oh, yes," he said. "T-backs were Zack's idea. Not Wanda's and not Velma's . . ."

"Why did you take this case?" she asked.

"Money."

"You're as bad as Zack."

"Not quite. I told myself that I was defending a freedom, but I think I was fooling myself. That is, until now. I think I ought to really do something for freedom—Bernadette's freedom to remain silent. There is still no way for a person to prove that she is not a witch. It took three hundred and fifty-nine years for Galileo's pardon. But even so, the pardon was done less on evidence—after all, the evidence had been in for three hundred and fifty-nine years—than on the fact that what seemed like a good idea in 1633 did not seem like a good idea in 1992. One generation's peace-symbol tattoo becomes another generation's upsidedown broken cross."

* * *

They heard the kitchen door open. Bernadette was returning with Daisy. Daisy appeared in the living room and went into her heading-dog stare and stalked Bayard from the front door to the living room sofa. "Can you call off this animal?" he asked. He felt decidedly unwelcome.

"Daisy is a *her*," Chloë said, gently taking Daisy's collar and making soft clucking sounds. "It's not a good idea to show fear."

"Fine," Bayard said. "Because what I'm feeling is terror."

Chloë smiled. It seemed like such a long time ago when she had said the very same thing. "Daisy's really very gentle," she said quietly.

"That's what they all say."

Chloë smiled again. She made more soft clucking noises in the direction of the dog, and Daisy lifted her head. Chloë said, "You can pet her now."

Bayard hesitated. Chloë said, "You don't have to, but Daisy will remember that she offered herself to you, and you refused."

He gingerly patted the top of Daisy's head.

Chloë said, "Bayard knows everything, Bernadette, and he's your lawyer now. I told him everything."

"Everything?"

Chloë nodded.

"Well, actually, Bernadette, I haven't been able to tell him how you got Daisy to follow you out of the warehouse when Jake died."

Bernadette sighed. "I can't tell him either. When I went into that warehouse. I had no idea that Daisy would allow me, and no one else, to touch Jake. If I could explain everything I ever did and everything that ever happened to me in my lifetime, I would be either too smart to live or too dumb."

25

When autumn came, the T-backers lost the first battle of the T-back war. COAT got the city council to pass a law that says no T-backs, not even in your own backyard, unless you are under ten years of age. The Reverend Mr. Butler's sermons are packing them in. Needless to say, he's developed a very large following. His Church of the Endless Horizon is filled to the rafters, and the reverend himself has become a consultant to other communities with a T-back problem.

Zack engaged another suit to help him fight city hall. In the meantime, he made so much money that he opened another commissary in Tampa. Wanda stayed in Peco to manage the business here. Velma went with Zack to start a T-back war there. When they make the news, they plan on sending the Reverend Mr. Butler all their tapes and newspaper clippings.

Tyler is enrolled in karate classes after school, and he is showing his talent for learning stuff.

At Bayard's urging, Bernadette quit working for Zack

and took a job working in his law office. She learned word processing and enrolled in evening classes to become a paralegal.

Bayard often helps Bernadette with her homework. They are not yet three-in-one, but they are working on it. Daisy is adjusting.

On her return flight from Peco, Chloë had time to think. She had a lot to think about. She knew a lot that she didn't know before.

She knew that she no longer feared total immersion or hair contracts, the frizzies or finding them in the mirror. She no longer feared saying no to a slumber party or saying no to Anjelica and Krystal. She no longer feared feeling *one-third* or less than a third as she often had with them.

She knew the difference between being three-in-one and being one-third. She knew she returned to Ridgewood much more the *one* she was meant to be. Not entirely, not completely, but well on her way, and she knew she would sometimes take a long look in the mirror to find the face of Chloë.

She no longer feared Rollerblades or dogs.

She knew she was going to get a Labrador retriever. A black one with a wet nose. She knew his name already: Lorenzo de'Medici.

And when people would ask her why she picked such an unusual name for a dog, she knew she would tell them, "Because it is unexpected," or "Because it seemed like a good idea at the time," or she would tell them, "Because five hundred years ago in a city called Florence . . ."